DOG YEARS

DOG YEARS

DENNIS DENISOFF

PULP PRESS

VANCOUVER

Published by
PULP PRESS
Arsenal Pulp Press Ltd.
100-1062 Homer Street
Vancouver, B.C.
Canada V6B 2W9

The Publisher gratefully acknowledges the assistance of The
Canada Council and The Cultural Services Branch, B.C. Minis-
try of Municipal Affairs, Recreation and Culture.

Printed by Kromar Printing
Typeset by the Vancouver Desktop Publishing Centre
Printed and bound in Canada

CANADIAN CATALOGUING IN PUBLICATION DATA
Denisoff, Dennis, 1961–
    Dog years

    ISBN 0-88978-234-2

    I. Title.
PS8557.E54D6 1991   C813'.54   C91-091445-1
PR9199.3.D46D6 1991

Why, like a well-filled guest, not leave the feast of life?

—LUCRETIUS

If that's all there is, then let's keep dancing.

—PEGGY LEE

1

The map of my death had been spread out before me as if for a god or clairvoyant, a clearly foreseeable construct. It was never a bloody death that I desired in particular (so few Canadian lives now end in blood) but the spontaneity and immediacy that a bloody death suggests, the fever pitch, the fervor. The necessary usurpation of fear. And it is the usurpation of fear which I have managed to attain, even in my slow plod. It is fearlessness that has positioned me before this computer. We all know the power of fear, but I have switched alliances.

My death will be much the same death most Canadians expect theirs to be, a death from old age, a death caused by the destruction of the body, emaciated and dim in a hospital bed, the colour of veins, catheters connecting the dots — following our ancestors through the bony gates of "Old Age." And it *will* be death from old age, premature death from aging—or so I choose to explain it. It is my computer after all. I control it. This keyboard, this monitor, this dingy screen and its spill of amber seeds, the seeds of the language. The ticking of my mind against the smooth, grey key-stones.

At one time, I actually had felt that language was within my control, that I used it. I see now that it has used me. Even when something enforces itself, adopts my life, demands my action, I lack the words with which to define it. Encapsulate it. Adopt it as mine. And I am not dangerous unless I do.

Death from age. Such a death, regardless of which definition of time is used (maybe it's the value of time that has placed me at this desk), is the only success. I found the pat equation 'Death = Success' soothing (as Larion once told me Montaigne had), particularly a few days ago, sitting in Sophie's Cosmic Café watching Paul enter, mementoes of secular success (the crispness of his Italian collar, his pleated handkerchief) clinging to him like leeches, though it was he who was sucking the power from them. He had aged about forty years in the two years that I had known him. Six dog years, but that doesn't sound any better.

How could he afford the clothes? He couldn't still be lecturing for the biology department. What might we learn from the VISA bills of the terminally ill? But Paul always seemed somehow 'well-dressed,' ordered, even when he wore nothing but swim trunks, limbering up to work-out tapes at the university pool. "Swiiing up. Swiiing down. 1-2-3-4. 1-2-3-4. Did you have a good time tonight boys? Yes, we—sure—did! Do you think the time is right boys? Yes, we—sure—do!" His silver swimming cap seemed tailor-made, clinging to his head like a fist, a heraldic shield printed on each side of it, along with the profile of a sphinx. And the bikini was a matching grey, and tight, to accentuate his abdominal muscles. This image has always struck me as attractive, with the grey hairs on the chest, the thick grey hairs poking out from under the cap, the wide eyes suggesting the cautious fear of the Velveteen rabbit. Sometimes, after exercises, he swam one or two lengths of the pool; usually he just clambered onto the bleachers to watch the other swimmers until he caught his breath, and then disappeared into the cedar-scented steam of the sauna.

But I was too shy for the sauna and we probably would not have met if the university mainframe had not been infiltrated by Medea. Or at least the virus guidebook calls it Medea, "an invisible force" (I have the book open in front of me), "which ricochets randomly across the screen, permanently erasing strips of text," etc. etc. It sounds like electronic whipping — strips of text. A few of the graduate students in

Computer Science were given the project of devising a de-Medea program and we created one that extracted the virus from discs, but we never figured out how to get it out of the mainframe. I de-Medea-ed Paul's private floppies a few times, and this almost led to us living together, but then there came the opportunity to study in the Soviet Union (literature, my minor). Adventure, anyway. Escape. The wild, blue yonder. Though that day at Sophie's, it had seemed to me that Paul was the one who had been pillaging across the waters. Much worse for wear, the eyes and hair were the only recognizable features of the man standing in the doorway scanning the clientele.

Such a striking contrast to the squawking flock of children that flew past him from outdoors, their shirts and skirts shifting swiftly around his emaciated body and fluttering noisily down the aisle and through the saloon doors of the kitchen—swing slap slap, swing slap slap. Paul. The silhouette of a matador. A young general on display. The pure white sunlight behind him, melting into the white street. Something unnaturally beautiful about the lines of the doors and the curve of his coat.

I was surprised to see his hair was fashionably cut (I don't know what I'd expected. Hair like a yeti's?), a razor-straight ridge tracing a line along the back from one ear to the other. His lobes, radiating in the afternoon sun, reminded me of my mother's fake pearl clip-ons. His slow feet scraped against the sandy, linoleum floor, but he ignored them, as if they belonged to somebody else, as if they had let him down. From his hips up, though, he still maintained a confident gait, a mannerism I had always thought affected until I saw him that day.

He held a couple of books I knew he would urge I show an interest in borrowing—more literature from the Christopher Street writers bewailing the plight of homosexuals as if all faggots live in Manhattan or want to, books showing how homosexuals could or do fit into the established structure of (white, American) society, books that rarely question the validity of social structure itself. I am not angry with their escapism. But this is life. Or more precisely, this is only life. And then there was his clutch purse, or I guess people in the fashion know call it something more exotic than "purse." Satchel? Pouch? Flesh-toned and limp, the bag reminded me of the belly of a lizard. What do I know about the bellies of lizards? What it reminded me of was a scrotum.

Paul's own skin, coated with bronzer, seemed like the flesh of a Ken doll. An impulse to kiss his scaly hands, moisten them with my spit, came over me and faded as quickly. Would Paul have seen the gesture as romantic (an attitude he considers sincere), or sentimental (which he considers false)? Or obsequious? For even now, aware of the misconceptions on which such desire is based, I could easily show him such physical affection. Since my crime (I will call it that for now), my definition of love has become personal. It never was before, having been predefined either by my parents or institutions or lovers—by all of this. At that moment, when I saw his gentle figure, I felt a brief urge to tell him I would measure out his medication and serve it to him, mix together the blueberries and yoghurt he always ate for breakfast, purchase the suppositories he told me he sucked on to alleviate the pain from the open sores in his mouth.

Everybody revels in loving the dying, the convenience of short-term martyrdom, and I am no better than anyone else (and by typing this I am suggesting that I am no worse). My mother found a scrawny kitten once, with transparent fur and eyes welded shut with mucous. It wailed incessantly and swung its head from side to side like an animated dinosaur in a horror flick, searching blindly for its mother, light, something. She fed it warmed milk soaked into a piece of cheesecloth, wiped its genitals with a warm rag to make it pee. I never expected the thing to survive and I'm sure mother hadn't either from the way she treated it afterward (worse than our other two cats). But years later, Colonel Yerosha was still around, now a fat, contented creature with kittens of her own impregnating the community. Mother's martyrdom had burdened her. Mother slogging through the freezing slush to milk the cow, and Colonel trotting between her gum-boots, mother kicking her aside, and Colonel flying into the snow bank like a chunk of dirt, a scarf yanked by the wind. The glazed acceptance of Wile E. Coyote waiting for the boulder to hit. Then trotting back into rank again between mother's plodding feet. Milk, milk, milk—its mind on an infinite loop. But this was not the same. There had been a hope of life in mother's nurture, a desire, however superficial. But then again, how am I typing these words into the computer, if not with some sort of desire?

I adopt the role of martyr too willingly, though not from any personal wish for atonement. What I did, I always knew, was socially wrong (don't expect me to call it a sin). I knew it was socially unacceptable each time I did it. But then, I can only maintain my personal perspectives since society has annexed me and, from my personal perspectives, social attitudes are less than inapplicable. Larion, over tea at midnight, always so official in his ESL, "Communal consciousness is necessary, since society defines itself through alienation. Society depends on discernable differences, on meaning, on those who do not accept these differences." And me, too absorbed in life to see the homophobia in his words. I should not have begun this entry with explaining why. With vindication. There should never have been any such desire.

If one saw the massive change in Paul over just one year, could that person still articulate Larion's defence for discernable differences? Or had it really been just one year? Though only forty-five years old, he looked sixty and carried himself as if he were eighty-five. How old is Paul really, if AIDS is drying the body, this icon of the night-life faggots, while his youthful romanticism persists defiantly? Sybil reversed and so much more surprised, though less regretful.

That day at Sophie's, he reminded me of the street mimes on Granville Island. That stilted shuffle. The white hankie which he flourished from the inside pocket of his suit jacket to dust off the seat across from me (Come on Paul, really!). But its silver wink successfully reinforced the thoroughness of his attention to fashion without having him come across as one of the tiring Davie Street queens, their self-conscious wardrobes becoming more flamboyant in proportion to each additional centimetre of flesh that melts from their chests to their waists. Fag: *sb.* 1. That which causes weariness; hard work, toil, drudgery, fatigue. And yes, I can see the bigot (the word seems so small on my monitor, as if some letters are missing. Bighout. Or Bigought. The Big Out). "What was the issue again?" I want to ask them, those garish queens. "What is the issue now?"

I have developed an affinity with the Wicked Witch of the West. I wonder, if nobody had killed her sister, would she have remained in her dark skyscraper with its chosen view, only bat-winged monkeys for companions? Would I be typing this? And what about the monkeys? Are they now stealing and murdering to survive? Have they moved to New York? I probably feel a stronger affinity towards them. They now have never existed. Popped like blisters in Dorothy's twisted mind.

This sense of being forced out into the open, forced to be a social counterfoil, to define an identity, a history, this has also worked to entrap us. Paul has often commended the flamboyant individuals who had the courage to flaunt their desires, but that is his history and not mine. That is history and I don't have any. For Paul, history is recorded as before and after the Stonewall revolt; for me, history begins with AIDS and AIDS is still here. What I mean to say is, history ends with AIDS.

Right now, rereading these last letters glowing amber in the night, I sense my intent, my desire, encapsulated yet undefined. By attempting to explain, am I trying to subsume it, defeat it, what the big boys have tried to do to us? The undefined. "Society," he said, "depends on discernable differences."

I don't think I have ever been within history at all—surgically removed, aborted, before birth. A patriarchal pill. It is this viewpoint exactly that allowed me to commit the crimes I did. Their word, not mine. Their world. This viewpoint may be egocentric but I'm sure it's a viewpoint each individual has. My actions were not in the least abnormal. On the contrary, they were the most logical gestures in my subversive existence, as short as it has been so far. I am twenty-seven. This is a digression. I digress from my own reality.

The reality was the image of Paul sitting down and smiling. The reality was the polish of his long teeth, made all the longer by his receding gums (a process I'm not sure is associated with AIDS). The reality was my own embarrassed grin, my glance downward, my noticing his fingers were poised to be clasped and my clasping them, rubbing a thumb along the back of his hand, as slack and smooth as an eelskin wallet. I had thought, at the time, that this was what he had wanted me to do and it irritates me that a person with AIDS, even Paul, becomes nothing more than a "person with AIDS" within the etiquette of society. The fact that people with AIDS are not dead but are dying may be too obvious, perhaps, too familiar for others to classify; it would entail re-classifying themselves, removing the deception of their own immortality. I would have preferred to discuss anything but this plague with him, but I had also classified him and so I found myself pouring forth my sympathetic bile.

"You've become a saint in the last two years," he replied. "Or at least a martyr."

"I think martyrs are worth more on the market, though I guess it depends on which saint you're talking about."

"St. Luke. St. Denis."

"St. Sebastian. St. Jean of the Rose."

"St. Ring-me-up!"

"St. Op in the name of love."

This attempted humour was inadequate and I was relieved when our waitress finally appeared. Swing slap slap, swing slap slap, the clutch of children tugging on her skirt and jumping on her toes while she took our order. Orange hair, black glasses, and the initials JC curly-Qed over her breast pocket. They couldn't all be her children but she let them tag along as if they were. Mother Goose. One of them managed to unclasp the tacky crucifix which hung from a chain around her neck.

"Hey, give that back or I'll slug ya." The girl, startled, handed it back to her and ran into the kitchen. "It isn't real gold," she told us, slipping the cross into the pocket of her blouse. "I'm not sure what it's made of but it's full of some chemical, linimite or something. My mother's Bulgarian. I used to have fainting spells, but the linimite balances me out." She winked at Paul (he's a regular), took our order and screeched it across the room to a plump waitress who stood smoking in the doorway of the kitchen.

"Get it yourself, Jude baby," drawled the curly haired waitress.

"What do the initials stand for?" I asked.

"I'm Johnny Cash's illegitimate daughter. Excuse me," she said, "I hear the train a-comin'," and all the children followed her into the kitchen except for two Greek boys, about eight years old, who stood winking at Paul and snickering into each other's collar bones (I had wished I was one of them). All these displays of nonchalance grated against the subtlety with which I had intended to deal with his condition, especially since I realized that Paul preferred the waitress' brashness to my clumsy sensitivity. "You make me feel like Diana Ross in *Mahogany*," he said, "or is that before your time?"

Jude had been here during his deterioration. It was more difficult for me to recognize the 'Paul' in him than for her, since I hadn't seen him for a year. Well, truly only about a month since he had met me at the airport, but the gathering of my wife's luggage and souvenirs (a brass samovar, three crates of Georgian wool, and half a dozen life-size matrooshki) left Paul tired and wheezing, so our reunion was cut short. He went home to rest and I used four taxis to deliver my possessions to the West End apartment Paul had rented for me and my wife.

He reminds me of an egg-timer, fragile, full of sand, and ready to be tipped over. The day I left, he had appeared so virile. I never even knew he had AIDS until I was in Kiev. He'd written me at the dormitory the same day as my departure. It took two months for the flimsy missive to reach my freezing hands. And winter had set in prematurely.

The letter was covered in black powder because it was Hallowe'en and my floor monitor had dressed up as a zebra. "Here, for you," she wheezed (her asthma was acting up), flicking the envelope into my palm as if it was a conditional leave. I thought she was giving out invitations to Foreign Film Night, which apparently had been suffering from poor attendance (not surprising since the cinema library contained only a few French war films and news reels on the industrialization of places like Kamchatka and Mongolia). I stuffed the slip of paper into the pocket of my overalls (Oxana, a student who lived across the hall from me, had dressed me up in her father's railway gear) and forgot about it until the next morning.

Hallowe'en was being recognized that night for the benefit of the foreign students, most of whom were from Africa and had never celebrated the day before either. Oxana had invited her friend Marina to the party as well and introduced me to her with what I mistook for the knitted grin of a matchmaker. Marina was not dressed in costume but she struck me as exotic regardless, in her black shirt and sheer, pink scarf which accentuated the clarity of her cheeks and aluminum eyes. Her gaze had that constant glimmer of hidden wisdom which I find so irritating in children. Her neck was so pale, it seemed that, if the light were right, one could see through it, and the thin vein crossing over her left temple was the exact same greyness as her eyes.

She had brought her brother, Larion, with her and I have described Marina first so that I would not have to go through the agonizing pleasure of remembering him in physical detail, agonizing even now. (This attitude is all I have.) I will type that he looked much like her except that his eyes were green rather than grey and he wore his hair parted on the side and greasy which, because it meant he was unaware of his own beauty, made him more attractive. He was wearing overalls, like me, but no shirt. I don't know what caricature his costume was supposed to allude to, half naked. At first I thought he might be dressed as a farmer but I know now that Soviet farmers look more like miners or soldiers than the farmers I've known in Canada.

I found it difficult to maintain a conversation with either of them, my third eye constantly dragging the other two down to the brass buttons which lay against the stiff, greenish-pink nipples, like tarnished pennies, on his hairless chest. I had never seen grey veins or green nipples before and I found the brother and sister captivating, like characters from a Ukrainian fairy tale. Ice deities. I wondered if my own skin would have been the same colour if I hadn't lain on the Vancouver beaches every summer under the ominous gaze of the Lions (they're called the Lions but I can't see it; to me they seem more like dormant volcanoes. If they must be animals, then hermit crabs).

Oxana, who received second prize for dressing up as a

garlic bulb, had to spend the entire evening sitting on a stacking stool with pieces of yellow cardboard stapled to it. She found a chair for me and placed it beside her throne but I really wanted to be talking to Marina and Larion. The other royalty was no more captivating than Oxana; on her right sat a greasy boy dressed as *The Book of the Dead* (Third Prize) and, on her left, a woman with well-defined muscles and bad skin who was dressed as a manned military satellite and who kept sneaking off to guzzle vodka through her fuselage (First Prize). Oxana's costume fell apart early in the evening and, while *Book of the Dead* mumbled insults at her for scratching his cover, and she and Satellite struggled to retwine the structure of chicken mesh and clothes hangers, I took the opportunity to leave.

"What records have they got here?" (I had to ask them *something*.) The Grateful Dead had been playing on the ancient gramophone all night. I use the word gramophone even in this era because of a questionnaire my sister and I had found once in the local paper. To enter all we did was complete a series of sentences:

On Sundays, the family drives into the country
for a _____ .
We have four months for summer _____ .
Put the record on the _____.

There were about ten questions in all and, from this, the editor of the newspaper would deduce our "intelligence age." We mailed our responses and a month later the replies came back on beige bond with a gold pin-stripe trim, our intelligence age centred on the page in fancy swirls. My sister had an intelligence age of twenty-four, which delighted her, since she was only fourteen, one year older than me. My intelligence age turned out to be sixty-seven, because I had said "vacation" rather than "holiday" and "gramophone" rather than "record player" or "turntable." She tried turning my little victory against me, saying it meant I wasn't "hip," while I, for years, continued to exploit her displeasure; "I hope we can bring a gramophone on our next vacation, don't you?" Stuff like that. If I hadn't been so catty then, maybe she would come to see me now.

I don't recall what Marina, Larion, and I talked about as we sipped our beers and rifled inattentively through the albums stacked beside the gramophone: foreign students, the lack of classifieds in Soviet newspapers, the latest murder in Hero City Park. Every half hour or so we went onto the patio so Marina could smoke away from the monitors' chastising gaze. The students didn't seem to care if a woman smoked, but it was the monitors' unspoken duty to rectify any such social faux pas. It must have given them a sense of authority.

The siblings' skin was glossy in the cold, like the scales of a trout. The Grateful Dead continued to crackle on the gramophone inside until, at about midnight, the machine broke down and everybody clustered together on the cots lining the walls of the room and sang Ukrainian folk songs, arms over shoulders, cheeks against cheeks, each voice searching desperately for another to harmonize with. Just like a university brochure on dorm life.

> *"We hear our soldiers' footsteps*
> *returning o'er the snow.*
> *Or maybe not. Who in fuck knows.*
> *Maybe so. Who in fuck knows."*

I never knew Ukrainian well enough to sing so I spent my time flirting cautiously with Larion on the balcony, but he showed no response. White goose bumps from the cold, but no response to me. I concluded that talking him up, bumping my knee against his calf, leering drunkenly at his green nipples, tactics I had assumed were universal, may not have been interpreted as invitations in Soviet society. Yet another language to learn. Linguistically over-burdened and too drunk for battle, I decided it was time to leave. No use being a slut on our first night.

Marina and I made arrangements to meet at the family dacha eighty kilometres out of town, so that I could help her with some translations. Larion was to accompany me on the trip, to ensure that I acted like a citizen (foreigners weren't permitted outside a fifty kilometre radius of the city). The train ride was the focus of my journey. The means as the end. Though I guess you could always turn around, go back, and do it all again. It's always such a surprise when the train enters the station and you aren't ready to disembark.

2

It wasn't until the next day, in the middle of helping Andrei inflate a soccer ball, that I remembered the envelope. I'm surprised that I had not recognized it as being from Canada the night before as it was my first letter from the homeland. Actually, the envelope contained a postcard of John Donne (sexy man) in his funeral shroud. Besides Paul's test results and a belated Happy Birthday (October 18), there was nothing engaging in the note or, if anything else was of interest, the interest faded into the smudges of zebra paint which I had transferred onto the back of the postcard.

The news itself did not alarm me, though Paul had not shown signs of deterioration prior to my departure. Instead I was overcome by a sense of bitter wholeness, that Paul's getting AIDS was somehow an obvious summation of his life-long attitude. It is not my intention here to suggest that Paul asked to be infected or had snubbed the advice of friends and doctors. I really don't know. Rather it seems to me he has lived life too confidently by society's standards, good things had come his way more readily than for others. His testing AIDS positive was a morbid counterbalance to the lack of disillusionment and failure in his, prior to AIDS, too consistent existence. My demand for logistics was still unquestioned back then.

His life reeked of *Reader's Digest*. "He had everything anyone could ask for—a career, a wife, two darling children . . . ." Except the crux of the biography is that Paul had no wife, or kid, no house in the suburbs, no hibachi or self-recoiling lawn hose. And he hadn't wanted any. His story could have appeared only in a gay version of the magazine's "Drama in Real Life" section. Or in "Life's Like That." That would be gay. Feeling I had come to terms with my own situation, Paul's news did not depress me but only made me wish that I could help him in some way, some relevant, real way.

Though Andrei had heard of AIDS, he felt that, "since the Soviet Union pre-tests all foreigners," there was no need for him to be concerned. When I informed him that I had not been checked, that actually only two out of the sixteen foreigners who had entered the Soviet Union with me had been tested upon arrival, he told me that that was no concern of his either since the Soviet Union had some of the best doctors in the world. He then recalled a news short we had seen recently in which a process of fiber-optic orthodontics for the elderly had been perfected in the Republic of Irkutsk.

"And what about the laser. And your contact lenses," he went on, excited now. "You can't forget contact lenses!" The big news in Soviet science at this time was the invention of a contact lens that would never have to be removed, being biologically grafted to the iris, stitched on with membrane from the cornea. The only drawback was that the pigment of the iris was destroyed, the entire eye becoming white except for the pupil. The big black hole. The big out. Rather than patients refusing to go through with the operation, people without eye problems were asking to have it done. It had become fashionable. White-faced, white-eyed Slavs. The invention was a success.

"AIDS is basically a blue disease. And I'm not gay. Valentina and me have been going out for over six months, so what's the worry?" Blue = Gay. Blue as a beach ball. Blue as violets. Blue as a bluebird's iris. "Don't it make your brown eyes blue?"

"Nobody is gay in the Soviet Union," I replied, trying to force him to admit his false assumptions, a feeble tactic which he easily circumvented.

"Yeah, some people are gay. But the government doesn't recognize this because it isn't important, whether a person is gay or not."

"Don't you think gays have got a different sensibility than other folks, their view may not fit whatever the government defines as typical? What about yours?" I had not opened the door of my Soviet closet and the practiced confidence of my rebuttal seemed to make Andrei wary. He was sitting on the edge of his cot, shining the soccer ball with the cuff of his shirt.

"If they want to go to the lake and fuck each other's rosies, it's none of my business. Hero City Park is open to everyone. But the government isn't going to waste its money catering to the sexual preferences of a few citizens." Ring around the rosy, pocket full of posy. Or, as Paul pronounced it, poesy. Maybe his version was correct. Regardless, the conversation was going in circles. Nothing either of us hadn't heard before.

Except for Andrei's use of the word "citizens." It almost compensated for his apathy. The sense of official bonding which the term evoked suggested that, regardless of his apparent disdain toward fags, Andrei had no intention of excluding them from the struggle of the working class or from sharing the victories of the collective. That would be the name of the first Soviet gay bar. Not "Buddies" or even "Comrades," but "Citizens." *Grazhdani*.

At the time, I was not aware that Hero City Park was the largest park in Kiev, or that it was also known as Park of a Thousand Lakes. Though covered in trees and ponds, the park seemed void of wildlife. There weren't even many people challenging the minus whatever weather. I passed a swish in a skidoo suit who reminded me of my Auntie Margo. Margo could make mother leave the room just by picking her toe nails with a knitting needle or discussing her sons' circumcisions. My mother also disliked her because she left lipstick on her cigarette butts and wore cat eye glasses with rhinestones in the corners. The fag's glasses were the same fake walnut as Margo's, without the gems. He also had the same walk, a shimmy that, while exaggerated in the lower part of the ass, left the upper section stationary, like the broom of a curler. I waited until he was well ahead of me (the forest was deciduous, letting me see for some distance) and then followed, hoping for a lead to the Lake of Fags. After wandering for an hour or so along icy paths that intersected, split into more paths, and then later converged only to split up again, it became clear to me that he was cruising, probably me, since the only other people we had encountered were a few skaters and two spindly war veterans looking for something in a snowbank. I let the swish lose me. They had to be so cautious.

The sun had begun to cast its dull orange glow when I finally admitted defeat to the oppression of the government; if there were any roses in the garden, they were too thoroughly subverted for me to sniff out. I sat on a bench and watched the skaters, students from my dorm which I, at the time, did not know was just over the ridge. I picked at a wart between my left index finger and thumb, counting the dark speckles which signified the number of roots. One of the skaters glided over to me and as he drew closer I realized it was Larion, which was too much of a coincidence to please me. Had he been assigned as my personal shadow? Had he been following me while I had followed the swish around the park? Did he know what went on in this park, what *apparently* went on? I acted blasé though the warmth of his grin and the perfectly round spots of colour on his cheeks made it difficult.

"We do not do that in the Soviet Union," he said, indifferently stirring eskimos, Maldavians, and the hundreds of other ethnic groups into one homogeneous bortsch. Is this what they call them there, eskimos?

"Do what?"

"Sit on park benches that are covered in snow."

"Actually, we don't do it in Canada either unless we're melancholy."

"Are you melancholy a lot in Canada?" The strange structure of the question made me wonder whether "melancholy" meant the same thing in Russian as it did in English. Did he want to know if I was often melancholy or if Canadians in general were a melancholy bunch? He was dressed like a character from one of those CBC family movies about a small town hockey player with premature arthritis. A black scarf was tangled around his aluminum neck (it had no actual colour, just a dull, metallic glow) and hay hair jutted out from a toque with the word EXPO printed around the ridge four or five times in boxy, red letters. Paul would have laughed aloud at the get-up, but this lack of fashion consciousness only drew out my respect. It was as if his clothes were not there; working against the social definition of beauty, they made him all the more handsome. He stood naked on the lake before me, too close to be an apparition though I toyed with pretending he was one.

"No. We aren't melancholy generally. We have no time. I know some people on the islands who are melancholy, but then, maybe they're just introverted." I expected him to ask which islands but he didn't.

"When we are melancholy here, we like to be alone."

"That's why I'm here." The conversation was constrained. We had nothing to say to each other and, anyway, I only wanted to admire him. I could feel the snow seeping into my jeans but I could not think of any reason to stand up. We stared at the skaters for awhile but, still, there was nothing to say. Everything seemed commonplace in comparison to what I wanted to do, which was not rim him, or kiss him, or even touch him, but just have him stand about ten feet back from me on the lake, as naked as he was, steamy wisps slipping from his lips, clouding his cheeks, and the trees behind him. I wanted to see him skate, defecate, sleep, breathe deep. I wanted at that moment to be as distant from him as possible, observing. I wished we had not met yet, so that I could appreciate him as an emanation. I wanted to follow the image along the snow-rimmed paths of Hero City Park, watch it glide over the ridges and then run to catch just one more glimpse, again and again. To freeze him.

Larion was not the first person I romanticized in this way. Nor was he the first person I considered murdering. After testing HIV positive, just before leaving Canada, everybody was attractive to me simply because I saw them as forbidden fruit. I hadn't told Paul about the test because I didn't want to worry him. I felt it was possible to hide my promiscuity and I still cared to, though now it's clear that he had not been monogamous either.

The fact that I am alive to write this suggests a failure to me. The fact that I am willing to write this verifies the irrational power of life. Will to live clearly seems to be an individual thing and, as Larion explained it, individuals are nothing without the strength of community behind them, propping them up and creating martyrs where no martyrs really exist (though he was discussing social development and I am thinking about social stasis). That last sentence sounds like a line from the intro to *Star Trek*.

The dead seem to be singled out, squashed individually under the heavy boots of the community, in order to be kept manageable. All accounted for, Sir. That must be why mass graves horrify society; the individual members are out-numbered. One at a time, anything can be done with the dead. Andrei had told me that in the second World War, the Kiev soccer team had been shot en masse by a firing squad for defeating a team of German soldiers. All the victors laying about the bloodied field. This was somehow more horrific. Oh my fucking God, they are all falling down together, before our eyes. Husha, husha. . . . Or something like that. One big tombstone for the bunch of them. I read somewhere that the Incas used to sacrifice their best athletes to the gods. It was an honour. Maybe this is how some of the homosexuals with

AIDS perceive their situation, in order to accept it — AIDS as a medal for their service in the 70s. Their purple hearts. Unlike those pet cemeteries in the United States, with a tombstone for every mangy cat and dog. And in Japan, the graves suspended above traffic intersections. Keeping the personal, individual — without glory but also without social grief. When I die, I want to be buried under the Lions, with a stone on my grave so huge that it would take a million people to move it in place. I do not want my body cremated. I want to rot in a compost heap.

Having redefined my death as ominous, it was possible for me to define my relationship with Paul as terminating upon my departure. Upon leaving the terminal. I really did not expect to ever see him again. When I received his letter, besides the new sense of wholeness, I felt an amusing displeasure that he had AIDS but was still alive — people dying unexpectedly, people living unexpectedly. The fickle humour of death had begun to grate against my mind.

Kiev gave me an opportunity to redefine the value of my short life. Since euthanasia was an accepted practice in the Soviet Union, there was solace in the hope that I would not have to go through the humiliation of losing control of my body. Also, and this whim was minor, I saw the chance of myself being a medical wonder in the communist world as a last opportunity for divine infamy. My name on one of those plaques screwed to the park barbecues. Or have I not mentioned those yet? I have to snicker at this idea now of course. It was well before my coming to terms with death and murder. Initially, my biggest worry was that my friends in Canada would have to watch me die. Even after I had given up, their self-distancing would force them to maintain hope throughout the lengthening ordeal, the disconcerting stretch of time. The long, painful, impatient, insincere breaking of bread. Companions, could you share my pain? (Sigh. "Oh, finally.")

3

It was not my test results themselves, but something to do with Canada that made me initially avoid sex. I told Paul that my anxiety over my departure had made me physically ill (not an all-out lie) and that abstinence from any form of affection was my method of dealing with the loss of his fuck. But considering the situation now, my abstinence definitely had something to do with home. Canada — you prudent nation. The fact that my mother lives here. Or that Canada seems defeatable. Unlike the Soviet Union, with its bloodless pride and loins of steel. One might think that this solid image of the USSR should have crumbled with the chaos at the Moscow airport when I arrived but, regardless of the rough edges, it didn't. Or was it that having suddenly found Russia in my lap, I could not see it? Unable to create any new image, or destroy any previous ones. The commotion of relocation disallowed any sort of conceptual redefinition.

Or could it really have been the stolidity of the architecture, which varied immensely but always impressed me? My first Soviet building was the airport. And it was raining, so there was no time to admire the exterior. They (who?) led us to some plastic chairs with the arms cracked off in the airport cafeteria, 'Chez Polski,' where we waited for our baggage to be located. Cream walls, cream doors. Captain and Tennille, of all people, crooning over the speaker system, "Muskrat Suzy said to Muskrat Sam. . . . " Me, reading Rowlandson's account of her capture by the Indians. "There was one who was chopped into the head with a hatchet, and stripped naked, and yet was crawling up and down. It is a solemn sight to see so many Christians lying in their blood, some here, some there, like a company of sheep torn by wolves. . . . " And Toni Tennille sings, "Muskrat Lo-o-ove." What luck to have had a wolf to tag it to! What if you all simply fell, Mrs. Rowlandson? Not to diminish your pain, but what would *that* have meant?

Two plump women in aprons and kerchiefs fried potatoes behind the counter. The large needle-point sign framed above their heads read, in English, "Roses are red, my love. Violets are blue. Sugar is sweat, my love. And so must you." A gift from some well-intending tourist? The clock informed us of eternal midnight. Or maybe high noon, show-down time.

We spent the wait sleeping in our chairs, eating bread, and throwing slices of meat at the walls of the trash can. Gutturals and labials bubbled from the door to my right (and every so often, a Carol Channing squeal of delight). Our luggage was finally brought out, various pieces of clothing still hanging from the baggage and a couple of zippers broken. We were all missing our walkmen (walkmans?). My razors, my leather gloves, and my condoms (even when leaving Vancouver, I had not wholly understood my new authority) were also missing. Two of the Canadian women, seemingly chosen at random, were taken into the medical office and given on-the-spot AIDS tests. Maybe they hadn't packed any condoms.

Fluorescent tubes of light. Squat support columns. Fake, cream archways. One got a sense it was all about to press down, like a giant waffle iron. And it was still pouring when the P.R. character shuffled us into a van, which drove directly to the station so that we could catch the overnight train to Kiev. Moscow wanted nothing to do with us capitalists and our wicked ways. The train station was my second Soviet building. Pungent with exhaust, hot oil, and sweat, it seemed like an industrial version of the Crystal Palace (my image of it, that is). Open and delicate, yet somehow very serious with itself. It was teeming with day trippers and unattended children. The clicks of a million knitting needles as the thin rain continued to pit the tin and fiber-glass. Stalwart attendants in ill-fitting suits shuffled back and forth with luggage carts, casting clips of language into the air.

I had begun to recognize the Slavic features I would find so attractive in Marina and Larion, the metallic skin and lips, the undefined eyebrows and solid cheeks. Metal as stove pipes. Watching *The Wizard of Oz* with my high school buddy, Elroy Seguine-Reichertz. "D'you know the Tin Man's a fuckin' fag? Just listen to him." And I listened but did not hear a single incriminating word. "Not *what* he says," whispered Elroy, irritated, "how he says it." Passing on foozball after the movie and rushing home. Then, in my bedroom, reciting "In Flander's Fields" (the one poem I knew by heart) over and over into the tape recorder. Praying that I didn't (but already changing my voice, knowing that I must) sound just like the Tin Man. My voice — some sort of biological traitor ticking away, waiting to expose.

The Russian porters, with their confident steps, defined shoulders, tight but heavy lips, marching forward to claim their maleness. All these masculine Tin Men. An occasional glimpse of the curve of a collar bone beneath a loose T-shirt, the hairless skin stretched along the base of a sturdy neck, the unexpected pulse of a vein below a disheveled scruff of oily hair.

Such a vein first attracted me to the porter. He was not beautiful in any classic sense of the word, or even peculiar the way European models like Rossy De Palma are these days. Instead he was wan, with greasy hair and cheeks so ruddy you could see the crinkly vessels of blood like a map of rivers and tributaries. The crease in his forehead made him seem frozen in dumbfoundedness.

My first image of him was from behind, as he removed his shirt, though this is not to be taken as an excuse. I had wandered into the employees' car accidentally, or maybe in search of something, an adventure (my eyes caked with mucous). He was humming a tune my grandmother used to sing. Over eighty years ago this song must have warbled half way around the world, from the largest country to the second largest. And here it was, back again, immortally spinning through our dying bodies on some mobius trip.

The pale blue glow from the overhead light made his skin shimmer like that of some subterranean creature, some sublunar apparition. The vein just below his scruff pulsed as the tendons on his neck contracted and my mind was overcome with the same desire that would consume it when I saw Paul's scaly fingers — to moisten that flesh with my tongue. My erogenous zones have always been on other peoples' bodies. The desire to gnaw, to lick and suck those undefined sections. And the pleasure is never oral, but internal. To swallow the scent, the texture, the musculature (what a heavy, delicious word). To consume it so that it is within me; only then does pleasure arise. I make love with my eyes closed. If my eyes are open, it is something else. You don't know what I mean. By love.

I did not go faint but my stomach contracted and I felt more hung-over than drunk. It was a sensation that could only have been cured by either consuming the boy or leaving the room and forgetting him. So I stood there, trying to look leather, waiting for him to turn around and, on seeing his mottled face, the hair-thin scar under his left eye, my desire for him became even more intense. It was the same sensation that would swallow me when I saw Larion dressed in his winter parka and toque, that the boy was totally naked before me, unconcealed, unadorned. A book falls open to the page.

The fact that he did not seem to read the desire on my face made me more desirous, for not even his expression accentuated his physical sexuality. I have never stopped on the street to catch my breath because somebody looked especially lascivious, or wore precisely pleated trousers, or because they looked at me; it is the physical beauty only that can be physically enjoyed. And it is through the consummation of my euphoria that any divine pleasure is derived. It would have been impossible to tell him my feelings since language itself dictates what it wants me to say. I am ineffable. One makes due with what one has. Language is what I'm made of. I just realized that this story is not being told in the order in which it happened. How much time takes what? If the dominant order has allowed me to conceive of speaking, then there must be a way for me to speak out of it.

"What are you looking for?" he asked, in the brusque tone of familiarity Soviets reserve for each other (my foreignness had escaped him).

"Sorry. This is the wrong car." The train whistled, "Too soo-oon, too soo-oon!" It was necessary to distance myself from him. There was no way to know how to speak to him without words. It would have been satisfying simply to have watched him, as if *I* were the emanation, his angel. Now my only hope was to prolong our verbal communication as long as possible. One belt loop missing and the belt sagging casually to one side. "Can I just sit down for a moment?" If he would only continue about his business and I, the voyeur, could smoke and admire his indifference. Or should I justify my request and act tired? Like I have asthma. AIDS.

"Same to me."

I told him the title of the song he was humming, feeling nervous. Not because here I was, turned on and yet toting around this deadly plague. Once you find out that you have AIDS, it's not as if you never forget it. No, nervous because here I was with a beautiful man. An innocent anxiety. "The fox came that night to the farmer's yard, Where the ducks and the geese declared it hard, That their nerves should be shaken and their rest so marred, By a visit from Mr. Fox O!" All these wild dogs.

"Are you Latvian or something?" he asked, taking off his undershirt, the unworshipped muscle along his rib-cage stretching like a cat in the cool light. His bangs swung fast over his face, long spikes of shadow scraping his right shoulder. And that wonderful steady nervousness, that incurable, innocent pain in the gut. Feeling so beautiful just by looking at him.

"No, Canadian. I'm a student in Kiev." In the background, the incessant clicking of the train on the tracks, like the tail end of some film footage spinning on an unattended projector. I crossed my legs and took out my pack of Players Lights, offering him one. The nails on his disproportionately large hands were splintered and rimmed with grease. His lips trembled as he lit his cigarette and mumbled simultaneously. Something like *golob* or *lyubov,* or maybe *goluboi*—blue, but my mind is probably just imposing this. I wonder now, for at the time I hadn't known the connotation that blue carried in the Soviet Union. He might have been planning our later meeting all along.

"I've never heard those words. It's an army song," he said in Russian. "Our boy has left from the farmer's yard, He's off to war where the life is hard, nuh-nuh nuh-nuh nuh-nuh-nuh nuh-nuh, And a kiss from Grandma Anna." Someone's words had changed. But something more important was still there, the synapse of communication, the rhythm of hope was still there. In the year 2070, someone in a drunken bar shouts, "One more time, Sasha," and swills his beer while the guitarist tunes his instrument and begins to play.

We smoked our cigarettes while he changed his clothes. I thought about whether I held my cigarette masculinely, something I hadn't worried about in years, but here, in this butch country. . . . I resented the fact that, because of AIDS, quitting smoking could no longer be a concern for me. My legs were crossed at the knees and I uncrossed them. Would the Tin Man sound gay if he spoke Russian, lived in the Soviet

Union? Or in Spain, where everybody lisps? Could the Tin Man cross those cumbersome legs of his even if he wanted to?

He asked me my compartment number and, after I told him, said he would serve me tea that evening. His tone suggested that this was a fact, that he would serve me whether I wanted it or not, but it's clear now, after a year in that country, that he was simply assuming that everybody drank tea, and my compartment happened to be in his section. We ground out the cigarette butts with our heels. The unseen breeze lurking about our feet, swirling the glow of ashes, amber as the letters on my monitor. The sparks sliding over the glossy leather of his boots. My first foreign night. An alien country. And everything else so gloriously far away.

I returned to my car with a sense of divine predestination (my angel [or my mortal] serving me tea, appearing before the other three students in my compartment as a spectre of my conjuring). Of course, when he finally appeared, it was not divine at all. Both Fred and Tom had fallen asleep, and David was in the washroom lancing a boil, so it was only him and me, too close to admire yet too distant to consume. Fred began to snore when the train jolted, and the two of us stepped into the hallway and made our way to the space between the two cars, where passengers were allowed to smoke.

The desire which my arrival in the Soviet Union had brought up in me, like a clipping of memory from some misplaced computer file, was fighting all this time against my awareness that my body carried the plague, that I had slipped this immense force into the confines of one of the most powerful countries in the world. It is not always clear to me what side I am on; is AIDS such a detriment or is it a new weapon? I don't know. Thinking about it now, it's easy to acknowledge that life is no great thing, yet it amazes me that then, on that train, I was already able to see the glory of death, only a few weeks after having been diagnosed. I am trying to keep in mind, while typing this, that my preferred position has made it easier for me than it is for most people to put life into context. Others have not been blessed yet with the realization of death's grandeur. And it is clear to me that I am making enemies. But think about that. Hopkins had enemies too. "Why should their foolish bands, their hopeless hearses, blot the perpetual festival of day?"

Enemies are no big shit. I used to think of Shelley dying at twenty-seven and it would upset me, imagining what this brilliant boy could have done if he had lived even one year more. But now it seems to me he could not have done anything more profound than die. And who would he be if he had lived longer: anybody *but* this Percy. They have given me yet one year more. And while we're at it, what about Chaucer working like a dog all his life, never clueing in that death was the ultimate success that wiped out any other measure of value? Oh, he must have figured this out, in his own way. It's there somewhere, that line about Troilus laughing at the mortals as they struggle within their own conceptions, but I can't find it right now. What a long, long list this could be. The breadth of people. It is because we fear life too much, that we wade so clumsily into the pool of death. We are so frightened of offending the living. Even Paul: "I know it sounds like a Susan Hayward movie, but I've been touched by a rather frightening lust to live!"

D-e-a-t-h. It clicks onto the computer with one hand almost, so casually. We say it only as our breath is expelled, never as we breathe air into our lungs. The breath of death. I welcome every sore, every sliver of scaly skin. Those animals that live longest — turtles, elephants — can't know they live longest. Or even that they've been alive. It would wreck everything.

There is something imbedded within language like wiring

which forces us to fear the dead and pity the dying. If only I could speak through a dog's brain; a dog who accepts life's process and shows such acceptance when dying. "They did very well without fork or knife, And the little ones picked the bones O!" To *not know* as a dog doesn't know.

"Then I took it of the child, and eat it myself, and savory it was to my taste. Then I may say as Job 6:7 blah blah blah." What we will do to stay alive, Mrs. Rowlandson; how new it all looks. What can be so tasty, what we do for liberty, and what we so quickly forget.

The metal cage shook as the train plunged far into the southern hills and we had to hold onto the door railings to keep from being thrown around. The clicking of the train was louder now. Foreground. As if we were within the projector, or strapped to the footage. The wind spilt into the compartment and tumbled about our ankles. The deep blue sky shone through the crack between the cars. Flat black phone poles broke the night with rhythmic thumps. The click of the keys on his belt loop.

When the train flung the porter against me, I was permitted to taste his greasy, brown hair. The smells of cigarette smoke, sweat, and cayenne. I remember the cayenne because mine had been taken from me at the luggage check in Moscow. The porter did not move away. An attempt at speech then, would have only led to stutters. He had dropped his butt but did not step back when he bent to retrieve it. And when he rose, he still stood as close to me. Some dim miracle, in its own way.

My desire for him had vanished from my mind; that is, it was not a cognitive thing. It was a part of us, as if it had always been. I was thinking about my love for him, and this word is used because language is used, but it was not love. It was a desire to consume, to consummate, to eliminate the duality of his existence, suck him into the wholeness of my death (which is life). To make him rise anew then, into life, to have him see it before him as I was seeing it. To pound it into him. This, all in one word.

My desire to have sex with him was based on this conviction to immortality, to destroy structure and thereby destroy the concept of death. When Larion and I were reading Montaigne, we came upon a line that felt so true to me that I had him read it aloud again and again. "Premeditation of death is premeditation of freedom. He who has learned how to die has unlearned how to be a slave." When I fucked Bogdon (for that is what he told me his name was), he was given his freedom, a freedom most people only realize when they are already dead. That night, as the gentle train cut a line across the deep blue wheat fields of the Ukraine and my three cabin mates slept heavily, alleviating the exhaustion of their lives, a seraph was being realized in a cramped, humble cubicle with only the raunchy clothes of porters as a bed.

And what has the mortal world lost? A porter, a wan boy who was once of no consequence to over ninety-nine percent of the population, somebody unknown until this was read. And who am I to speak? No one; I do not have to speak, do not have to say a fucking word. The click of keys. The steady click click clicks of the world. Like an unloaded gun. The keys of my keyboard are proving not to be keys to anything.

4

Blue, whether it be the deep blue Ukrainian night or the blue of a beach ball, is not a communist colour. And yet it has always been such a masculine, powerful colour to me. In the culture. But no, red, as in the street name, or at least ocher, the colour of the dormitory. My dorm on Krasna Armaiskaya Oolyitsa (Red Army Street — even the names of the streets demand respect) was the third building I had looked at in the Soviet Union. Toward the end of my stay in Kiev, when things were really upside-down, Larion asked, "Did you know that the Russian root for 'red' and 'beautiful' is the same?" And like a dictionary illustration he stood there smiling, two red spots like poppies against his cold cheeks. This is what I regret losing, these complete direct images.

The dormitory was a square building that resembled a giant cake box really, four stories high. But so cool and permanent with its rough cement walls and heavy glass windows. Heavy wood doors about twelve feet tall that pushed you in once you managed to open them. This image was reinforced by the squat granny who gave us our linen, speaking all the time through a mouthful of dough which she maintained by adding to it every so often from a loaf she carried in a shoulder bag.

Third Floor, Number 357. Who knows why I remember this, of all things? Andrei, my roommate to be, was in the country helping with the potato harvest. Instead of him, there were two geology graduates in my room who were supposed to have moved out but chose to remain as long as possible to avoid having to pay rent — free living quarters as long as they weren't discovered. This didn't present any problems.

My temporary roommates were Leonid and Leonid, one pale, the other dark, and both about twenty-five years old. The walls of the room were covered in Heavy Metal posters and a signed photograph of Sylvester Stallone. "You're a knock-out Annette! Love Rocky." The gramophone in the corner was playing Black Sabbath. I put my bags on the coffee table, which was covered in candle drippings, ashes, and a dog's skull with the stub of a white candle on its cranium like a tiny top hat. Actually, it was the skull of a rare species of wild dog from central Siberia. That's it, they were archeology students, not geology students. A grave robber, one of them called himself. There was also a fish tank next to the table, translucent with algae. A fat goldfish wallowed at the bottom with a clump of algae clinging to its tail.

It would be convenient if I could define a symbol as my own, but I can't. Nothing in 357 attracted me in that way, and to type that I wallowed like a fish, or became as lifeless as a skeleton, would not only be contrived but also a lie. I did not want to wallow. I have not grown thin. What do you imagine me to look like, sitting here, typing? Metaphors frighten me, make me scared to type, to suggest a type. I try to be more there than here, more re-experiencing the year than experiencing the typing, not stepping back to consider what's been typed. Every moment spent explaining this contradicts the argument, so I'll return to my room.

I got one of the three cots, and we shared the wooden table and the closet full of clothing and cleaning supplies. There were two French doors leading out to the patio, but the dark-haired Leonid warned me not to stand out there for too long because the previous year a patio on the top floor of the building had collapsed, wiping out the two below it. Nobody had been injured, but as of then people generally used their patios only as places to hang laundry or, in the winter, as natural refrigerators, since no electric ones were supplied.

I spoke English to them even though my Russian was strong, since an ignorance of their language would have been a plausible plea in case of any social blunders on my part. Unfortunately, the Leonids spoke flawless English and there was no possible way for me to claim miscomprehension. They became protective watch-towers for me, defining my position in society as well as everybody else's. Each morning I woke to find them already seated at the table, the sunlight sliding through the patio door, turning their hulking figures into ominous silhouettes. They sipped their Georgian tea and stuffed chunks of bread and cheese into their mouths ("The little ones picked the bones O"). Sometimes they read weight lifting magazines, sometimes comics. At about 11, they began taking turns lifting a stone the size of a bowling ball over their heads, Atlas 1 and Atlas I. When they were finally sweating, they would step onto the patio for a few breaths of crisp air. Steam rising off their shoulders as if they were Clydesdales on a Christmas card.

Awake by this time, I would join them in their trek to the showers. Proper communal shower etiquette, according to the Leonids, involved mutual back rubs and the throwing of scalding hot washcloths at your buddies' thighs. They were impressed by the girth of my legs (which suggested solid peasant stock) and dragged me to their sessions in the weight room at the school gym. I was never one for pumping iron and after a couple of half-hearted efforts on my part, they stopped inviting me.

On my second day in Kiev, they took me to see the movie *China Syndrome* because they wanted to ask me questions about Jane Fonda's hair. "Is it that colour naturally?" "Are there many women in America with hair like hers?" The next day they took me to see the rock band "Tractor" and, the day

after that, to a soccer game between the Kiev Dynamos and
the Ryga Tractors. The Dynamos won, which meant we had
to rush back to the dorm to shoot vodka and eat salted fish
out behind the Greek Orthodox church next door. Throwing
up was apparently the proper reaction because, upon returning from behind the priest's hut, both men hugged me and
slobbered on my cheeks, laughing so heartily their capped
and rotting molars showed. We spent a lot of time discussing
what was most attractive about women. They showed me
numerous black and white photographs of their girlfriends,
who were harvesting potatoes in the countryside, and took
me to more films starring women with thick red hair and
muscular legs.

The Soviet screen idol at this time was a singer by the
name of Alla Pugachova, a thirty-five-year-old with athlete's
calves who had three themes to her lyrics: love for her boy-
friend, love of the countryside, and the fact that she had only
two themes to her lyrics. Alla's big hit was "A Thousand Pink
Roses," and whenever the song came on the radio both
Leonids would leap up and begin strumming air guitars even
though the only string instrument in the ballad was a violin.

During this period, death (life) rarely entered my mind,
simply because I was too busy living. Life had proven itself
more repulsive than I had earlier thought. Whereas it once
seemed to be simply a void, a nonentity in relation to death's
divinity, life now appeared actually evil, working to distract
us from salvation. It's as if, in an effort to avoid death, we
immerse ourselves in living and this short term distraction
ultimately finds us meeting death unprepared, unapprecia-
tive, and unaware. Like cats which have fallen into a sewer,
clawing at each other in a blind attempt at salvation. Death is
our immortality only if we realize it. And here again, our pack
mentality. Divided we fall, apparently.

When the Leonids were kicked out of the dormitory, they
took their record player, albums, and posters with them, but

left me the dog skull and the goldfish, whose name was Motorhead ("Thank you, thank you so much"). On their last day, we got drunk, looked at photographs of Lana and Svetlana, and discussed what we found most beautiful in women (an issue we were in complete agreement on by now). These men, I did not love. They did not carry with them any appreciation for either life or death and therefore there was no reason for salvation. They were, in the traditional sense, dead to the world, and any efforts made to raise them above their dense senselessness would have been futile. One can only resurrect the living, the dead being fixed outside of this realm.

The Leonids had distracted me which, when realizing the true perniciousness of life, I saw as no casual digression but as a potentially nullifying development. The ease with which they had subverted my devotion frightened me. I was prepared to let myself die, and hoped that a return to lethargy would speed up my physical decomposition, but my health never waned. Adamant to falter, I would sneak out of the dorm at night and lay on the skating rink at Hero City Park until my fingers could not move and the tips of my ears froze, but, well, my solid peasant stock. . . . It only seems romantic in retrospect. At the time, I would have greatly appreciated being hit by a streetcar or run over by the funicular. This was a frantic counter-action, but the realization of my imminent termination led to my making conceptually pat analyses. Suicide was not really a feasible solution, since death had ordained my way. The best I could do was prod death along. Like the Greek Orthodox priest at the church next door to the dorm, I saw suicide as a sin, a challenge to the divine. These are religious terms but I do not believe in a god and did not believe in one while in Kiev. Death was my divinity but it was never personified in my view. How can you personify boundlessness? I even feel guilty for imagining it to be a giant gelatinous sphere encompassing the universe, pulsating like an embryo, something I'd seen somewhere before, my mother's womb perhaps, or an alien force in a re-run from *Space 1999*. The clearest description I can give of death is to say that it is a process, a constant, consistent consumption of everything and everything those things imagine and so on. An exponential consumption of everything including this definition I am keying in. Bones and all.

But if suicide was blasphemous, then so were my nocturnal escapades in the snow; all that I could do was continue living as I had before testing HIV positive. Even though I argued adamantly that my view on death was not religious in any traditional sense, I was sounding like a puritan, a zealot, though how this could be so, when there was nobody else to compare my devotion to, I don't know. One can only be puritanical in relation to the norm and, for me, there was no norm. I was the sole member of this religion, if I must call it that.

Gregory Maximovitch, the priest at the church, was the only person who ever heard my rants because he was the only one who took me seriously. Was it just a last existential fling really? For him? Afterwards he would instruct me, in a heavy Ukrainian accent (he was proud of his English), to redirect my fanaticism toward God, which he would define as loosely as possible so that it might fit my philosophy. Our conversations took place at night in a stone room with a dirt floor in the basement of his church. Here we could drink the blood while I bewailed the anguish my unfailing health was causing, without fear of interruption. Melodramatic, I know, but recognition was important to me at the time. Nobody is taught how to deal with death, so is it surprising that we fall back on clichés and movie images? Why am I writing this? Was this one of the stages of acceptance? It doesn't matter. I've skipped 'Denial' altogether.

Gregory Maximovitch would sit down on a bench, stare at the floor, call me "son," and bum another smoke, all the while mopping his dripping nose with a hankie. Though by the time he asked for the cigarette, he was no longer staring at the floor; everything changes before one sentence ends. If the words ever tried to keep up to the images, this would all just be a blur. These descriptions are more like one of those animated hockey flip cards that I got as a kid. Skat-er-swings-and-puck-flies-to-ward-to-ward-to-ward-me-whoa! Worn with boredom and half drunk, I would sprawl across one of the two sepulchers in the room and continue my now memorized rant for the final time that evening. Then Gregory Maximovitch would begin pacing the chamber, illuminated by the naked bulb dangling near the shut door. He'd often piss in the corner, but there was never that smell of confined urine in the room. Maybe its alcohol content was too high. Or maybe the place was too cold.

"Son. Dyearest. It's like dis." He would lean against the wall, pull in a heavy breath, and continue. His mouth shook a bit before he spoke, as if he were tasting these exotic, English words. He looked like a character in a badly dubbed movie. "Life is hard. There will be many problems for you along the way that you must look out for. . . . " (*Luke* out for.) "As there is for everyone." Though Gregory Maximovitch attempted a new line of argument each evening, his soliloquies always began with those lines.

"We aren't children anymore," he said.

"Uh-huh."

"But once we *thought* we were," he replied. "Let us ask perhaps what God and death have in common? Well? God and death are close. They are buddies. Where death is, there goes God. Where God's garden grows, there we will find death planting the seeds which will test the faithful. To believe in God, one has to believe in death.

"It convinces me, my son, dyearest, that you believe in death. Not just death, urk and that's it." He made a choking motion with his waxy fingers. "No, but death in the sense larger. Death as the inevitable. Death as the entry to heaven.

He who fears death, fears heaven. He who fears death is a sinner and will not find entry into temple of God." The priest glanced over to see if his speech had attracted me, then wiped his nose and took another drag of his smoke.

Seeing him there in the depths of that ancient church, altering the word order of his limited vocabulary so as to eke out yet another angle, speaking only in words, it became obvious how far away he was from any sort of awareness. A naked, trembling bulb. I could watch him and I did not want to. He knew nothing about society or death. He, himself, was as stone dead to salvation as the Leonids. He was not of this world or the other. I feel like one of those lower class clerks in Gogol's short stories, blundering about the plot for forty-odd pages as a signifier of the uselessness of existence. But that isn't me. I realize the uselessness; I do not signify it.

"And this is where you are wrong, son, dearest. You shouldn't disregard the Bible. Everybody I know is named after a saint. It is because garden of God is the ultimate salvation and nobody can forget that. Death is just the gate into the hereafter. But garden of God will be just like life under communism only better, more food, no oppression, no line-ups. You could parcels mail any day of the week. We will go back to the old calendar. . . . " Gregory Maximovitch's voice would dissipate into a mumble as he sat himself down again, day-dreaming about his ideal communism. Once he came around, we would go up to his hut at the back of the church, to drink tea and play chess (he could not follow checkers).

A narrow garden bordered his shed on three sides. It was covered with a slanted roof made of chicken wire and inter-woven with grape vines which managed to keep most of the snow off the garden. I'd puked in this bower before. At this time of year, the plot consisted of nothing more than hollow sunflower stalks, blown cabbages, and poppy seed bulbs like black knuckle-bones. Sometimes, if the chess game was forced to end, we would weed, picking at the soil with rusted spades, piling the white weeds like tape worms on top of the compost heaps. On warm days, we would drag the cot into the middle of the garden, and sit there, smoking cigarettes. Occasionally Gregory Maximovitch would bring a bottle of wine out as well but, since the days were cold, he usually preferred tea. He blasphemed the Leonids for having turned me on to vodka, though he had never, never tasted it himself. Often, we fell asleep there, amongst the hard clots of dirt and vegetation. Gregory Maximovitch needed the fresh air for his health. The Leonids, too, slept with the window open. Occasionally I would bring him my Russian assignments from the Institute and he would complete them over the week, even though I had more free time than he. All the time in the world.

During these visits, the priest's view of life and death and heaven and communism did not change much. If anything, he saw life as more agreeable and death as more mysterious than he had when we first met, and though speaking in opposition, I understood that my enjoyment of the conversation itself undermined my argument. We were like two monks in a forgotten catacomb, our separate persecutors having passed us by for dead.

Gregory Maximovitch had not worshipped me, but envied, yes. Envied my freedom. The church had pinched his mind and would not let loose. Life had become an allegory to him, an impossible attempt to recreate the power which consumed his brain. In itself, life no longer existed. Every piece of vocabulary bore its divine burden. It had become the awkward definition of religion as he had been taught it. And this functioned (shooting at one heron but killing the one behind it) just as well. This is what I was doing with Gregory Maximovitch myself, taking a shot in that rotting vegetable garden. And with the Leonids, taking a shot. And maybe, in a way, with the porter, I'll admit that, maybe with Bogdon. But not with Larion.

5

V8. A delicious blend of eight vegetables. Tomatoes, carrots, celery, parsley, beets, lettuce, watercress, and spinach, with salt and seasoning. This is what is written on the can I just got from the fridge. This is what I just downed, and I'm comfortable with that. I just downed comfort. Comfort is a fucked thing. Social comforts. Creature comforts. My comfortable understanding of death. It was comfort that forced me to stop seeing Gregory Maximovitch. For what I intended to be my final visit, I brought him a bottle of white wine, a pack of smokes, and my Patsy Cline tape ("Stop, Luke, and Listen? Is it gospel? Ha ha"). We sat in the garden, wearing our thick overcoats, moving the stubby chess pieces with our mittened fingers, until the sky turned grey. Though I never told him it was supposed to be my last visit, it must have been obvious to him. He seemed uncomfortable.

Death had become such an obsession under the guidance of that priest that to return my thoughts to the issue of AIDS filled my mind with a sense of political clarity. In relation to death, AIDS was trite. The final blue bodies of doctors and children rotting about the hospitals. Connect the rot. This is how I see it at this moment; usually the images are much more aesthetic. Anaesthetic.

The usual image is of myself dying at grandmother's because that is where sleep was most peaceful. The lap of death. Coarse wool blankets and the cool smell of chicken feathers. Two wooden chairs placed against the bedside to keep me from rolling off the mattress. The scent of mold somewhere within the walls. The taste of it, gritty on the roof of my mouth.

"Smell is the sense with the longest memory." That was my line in our Grade 3 Christmas play. I was a nose. Mother had made the costume out of chicken mesh and itchy foam, and father had spray-painted it pink. The paint had eaten pock-marks into the foam which kept getting larger and larger and father was worried the costume wouldn't last. Even then, I was decomposing. The class had written the poem itself. "Without our eyes we couldn't see. Without our mouths we couldn't speak. Touch is the sense that feels the best. . . . "

But for me, smell feels best, if that makes sense. An image of grandmother puttering around the kitchen in the morning, preparing breakfast, not understanding what has wasted away her grandson, but fighting it with her grandmotherly stubbornness regardless. Gora, the old Labrador, barking at the coyotes slinking softly down the hillside toward the chicken coop. The Lab of death. Our protector. The smell of coffee is a strong memory. Can one become addicted to a scent? Of coffee? Or to the image? And the smell of milk. Brown eggs, hard boiled, with stubborn bits of shit still clinging to them. This is all supposition. Grandmother was run over by a snow plow over three years ago. And it's not likely the new owners would let me in. "Hi, would you loan me your bedroom, the one with the view of the birches and the river?" And then have them find me, tangled in the sheets and blanket, blue and blue and white. My high school colours. "2-4-6-8. Who do we a-pree-she-ate?" How quickly does one turn blue? A sour, 50s blue. A twisted teal. Grandmother's laugh. Will my cock spray piss when I die? Or will it be too worn? It's not up to me to decide whether she is laughing now or not. But I can hear her laughing, laughing at my seriousness. It's funny, where I have searched out comfort — within the church, within the Leonids, within this text.

When one thinks of timelessness, one thinks of comfort, the endless years stretched out across some hazy horizon, that wrap-around painting by Monet. Yet, it is the clock which stops, not the one which keeps going, that actually addresses the whole concept. The worn out battery. The weaker tick-tick-ticker. Almost two whole months had passed, two whole *HIV* months, since my arrival in Kiev and I still had not actually befriended anyone. Therefore, at the Hallowe'en party, there was no choice but to monopolize on Marina and Larion (or to let them monopolize on me). Oxana must have realized what was going on but my conscious intentions were not as calculated as anybody else's. I was simply rediscovering the satisfaction to be found in physical beauty, now under the illuminating rays of death. There was no confusion between physical beauty and the beauty of life. I might have devoted all my attention to the institute, but the lectures were couched in communist propaganda, leaving no room for the romantic perception I preferred—socialism with a biological, rather than political, origin, the politics as organic to existence rather than a definition of social structure. The lectures were crushed by my personal renaissance. Passion and justification. Physical beauty was defined as the origin of existence, with death as the culmination of my appreciation (rather than death as the *origin*, which is how Gregory Maximovitch interpreted my rantings). Or physical beauty as internal and death as existence itself combined to create a presence, or essence, that was the source. Language is once again forcing me to use religious terminology or esoteric extrapolations that can really all be fused into one guiltless, all-consuming word — a word which does not exist.

Larion, not Marina, though the two seemed often inseparable to me, was the embodiment of this sublimity. My passion was fervently adopted, with me masturbating sometimes three times a day whereas just weeks earlier no sort of physical gratification was considered. My morning hard-on had been simply a digression from my ideology, some sort of puritanical test. But now my every thought was centered around a fusion of the physical and immortal. Sometimes I masturbated to the postcard of Donne. This enjoyment hadn't deterred my worship of death either, my mind confident that mortal history began and ended in death. This had nothing to do with necrophilia.

After the Hallowe'en party, my Friday meeting with Larion took on a passionate expectancy previously reserved for my death. He had taken on this mask of socialist decadence. I imagined him paler and more streamlined as the days of the week marched on, a sort of subterranean creature whose sole purpose was to swim across my mind.

On that Friday, I made sure my body was consciously unmarred by such vain accoutrements as those which adorned Paul that day at Sophie's. The chalk mark on my wool pants was not removed, for it made me less veiled. My black scarf suggested a romantic bond, since Larion had worn a similar scarf that day on the ice. My stupid, admirable calculations. Once again, my adoration of death had almost been displaced by a fascination for human life but, as I rose from the metro, the gust of winter air that shot down from the open door led me to feel that, though the biting sensation may have been nothing like the sensation of dying, the entirety of its envelopment paralleled the entire glory of death, which was the consummation of my physical adoration. I have dug out a quote from St. Theresa's *Book of the Castle Within* that was supposed to reinforce this sensation, but it's clear that it isn't dead on; my sensation could not be defined as pain. But then, she had to use her language; "The pain was so severe that it made me utter several moans. The sweetness of this pain is so extreme that one cannot possibly wish it to cease." To wish that sweet pain not to cease was an attempt to control the sublime, and it was such blind boldness that had led me to the petty depths of Gregory Maximovitch's church. Gregory in the dirt.

The wind rushed me like what then, if not death? A gaggle of geese? A cluster of children? Their healthy hands clasping my ankles, wrists, and neck, shaking the chalk from my pants, tangling the strands of my hair? No, for Andrei had given me a crewcut just the day previous. And kids couldn't have reached my head anyway. Angels perhaps. Something out of Walt Disney. Those dexterous bluebirds.

It is children I will miss most. Does this sound awkward? I can love your children. I *could* very possibly have my own, even now. Nothing is more possessive than the norm. Nothing is more disturbing than realizing one's own jealousy. Nothing more horrifying than the image of one's own mediocrity.

And how could I have realized my trespass then? How could I have felt mediocre, as we made our way toward the train station, me neither trying to admire him as an apparition nor making an effort to communicate my worship of him? Maybe on the train, but not then. Once we had purchased our tickets and were seated, my mind felt a mild relief. Just one week earlier two other Canadian students had been caught trying to go visit their relatives in a village outside the limited radius and their travel privileges had been suspended. This did not worry me so much because Larion's flat was in Kiev and it was Larion only who I wished to see. Had they barred my right to see him, on the other hand. . . . But at the time, such a repercussion for my actions was inconceivable.

The train was packed with farmers from the markets returning to their villages for the weekend, but we managed to find two seats beside each other near the back of the car. The scent of confined sweat and pickled eggs clung to my lungs. Chickens clucked underneath the seats and the aisles were lined with burlap sacks full of unsold potatoes, turnips, and pumpkins. An old, balding woman came up to us and asked if we wanted to buy some handicrafts (she did not want the hassle of carrying them back to the village and was willing to sell them dirt cheap).

"What's wrong with you?" Larion said to her. "What are we going to do with that?"

"Hey, five rubles for it," she replied, dragging the painted ladle across my field of vision like a hook.

"We've got our firewood, Granny. Get out of here."

Somehow the woman had recognized me for a foreigner. My clothes were urban, but there were others in the car dressed as urbanely as me. Some of the men even wore suits.

"It's your cologne," Larion whispered to me.

"It's not cologne. It's aftershave."

"Soviets don't wear cologne."

"I bought it in Kiev," I whispered back, irritated that somehow an earthly memento *had* managed to leech onto me after all.

"Soviets do not wear cologne," he repeated, in English. The granny, who had seated herself at the other end of the car, winked and closed her eyes. Why should she care about my destination? Why should anybody know my intentions? What did they want so badly to protect? What did they think I had?

"Straighten your face. She's gone to sleep and *you're* still squaring her over." I absorbed my grimace, feeling dejected. Larion must have sensed this for he rubbed his hand along my leg, down to the knee and back to the base of my pants pocket where he left it, with no sense of contrivance on his part. This gesture gave me a sort of giddy rapture. We were on an adventure. No, that's not quite right. The words "giddy rapture" glowing like neon on the screen remind me of those lines from a song by Nina Hagen, "I'm in ecstasy, gonna jump down my balcony. I'm in heavenly agony, wanna fulfill my destiny." And it was almost that giddy, but already (maybe instantly) there arose the dear pain of my expectations. Again the split moment of eternity is sacrificed. Even the clacks of the train vary one from the next. I craned my eyes but not my neck to look at his fingers with their rectangular nails and almond cuticles, not the fingers of a clerk or a musician. Fingers good only for stroking, active and passive.

Smoke poured from the huts as if from billows, as spills of farmers flowed out of the train at each stop. Instead of snow, there were dull, tilled fields of soil interspersed with leafless birch groves under the darkening sky. The train continued straight and flat, as if crossing a pane of glass or a frozen ocean. Entering an ice age. The first thing I noticed when Larion rose to get off was that at some point he had removed his hand from my thigh without me noticing. There was the hand a few yards in front of me and I wanted so badly to have it back. I type "have," knowing that you prick up your ears, but is it possessive, if it was offered? Is it murder if it is never defined as such? Were we leaving the train or entering the terrain?

6

The two of us walked through a gauze of fog along a road coated with a thin graze of snow. Slow, but our steps only brought us closer to the black box on the edge of the field, its harsh spark of light and the intrusion waiting within. Giddy giddy yap yap; Marina met us at the door (too soo-oon, too soo-oon) and led me by the hand to the wood stove, pushing her fat lips against my cheek and calling me by some animal diminutive. "You little chipmunk." "My frozen bunny." She was speaking English, stiff and twisted, so it was difficult to tell whether she was joking or not. She wasn't, I know now. And how we all could have used a bit of comic relief later on, instead of those months of grunts, nothing even liminal, just plain nowhere.

Marina mothered me the entire evening, topping up my tea cup, begging me to finish the last of the potatoes and eggs so that she could wash the bowl, offering to iron my shirt which had gotten wrinkled during the train ride. Mothered me like my mother mothered. What are these gestures doing on opposite ends of the world? She kept changing radio stations in search of entertainment, but all we could get out in the country was Moscow and Kiev. And static, lots of static. And on the television, either Moscow or a blizzard.

"Where is the book then?" I finally asked, having decided that Marina was simply being polite in not suggesting we work. "If we leave again tomorrow, then maybe it's time to start translating."

"It's here," she said, bringing a dog-eared copy of *Nausea* to the table (with the same servile manner that she had been using all evening), "but it can wait until tomorrow. For that matter, there's no reason you couldn't stay here until the cows come home. But on Sunday, mother arrives." Larion laughed. "I didn't mean it like *that*, you jerk," she snapped, but she was smiling.

"But there's the monitor back at the dorm who'll be waiting for me."

"She doesn't matter, you know. There's nothing they could do."

"There must be something. Suspend my travel privileges."

"But I'm moving into Kiev next week," she said, "so you won't have to come out here anymore anyway, and we could still go on day trips into the country. And who really wants to travel in the winter?"

Thinking back, I recall that Larion had not argued one way or the other. Maybe for him it was all inevitable. Of course it was. Everybody wanted it, but only he knew. There's something coercive in that passive confidence, knowing everybody's motives but not saying a word. Just laying on the divan, legs hanging over the edge, calves pressed taut. Grey work socks. Giggling at the television between mouthfuls of popcorn.

And me and Marina at the kitchen table, kilometres away, with our paper, our pens, and our text. Between us lay the phlegm-coloured book, interspersed with ink drawings of cobblestone streets and squalid buildings that alluded more to Dickens' England than Sartre's France. The sections Marina wanted translated were underlined in black ink. "Of course a movement was something different from a tree. But it was still an absolute. A thing. My eyes only encountered completion." But then Marina could not understand why a "movement" should be compared to a "tree" at all. It seemed irrelevant to me as well. And for her, "absolute" had always been an algebraic term. "Why the eyes in here?" she asked in her curious English. Though Marina is intelligent, her English often makes her come across as dim, or quaint. Missing verbs. Twisted terms. Did I sound as daft when I wasn't speaking *my* mother tongue?

Context was an irrelevant issue for Marina, who was concerned with the practicality of the exercise. "I don't have time to read the entire book. Why must I know the context? Can't you just explain quickly for me what is going on, give me a little context? Does it take place at sea?" After five hours, we had managed to translate most of the sections, in our way. The passages made little sense to either me or Marina, who had written all of our efforts in the margins of the book.

Larion had barely moved the entire time, only getting up to pee or to play with the television reception. He showed no interest in our work, and this flattered me. My nonexistence meant I was naked before him, as naked as he had been to me. Oh, but then maybe if he had seen me as someone just a bit more exotic, a bit more delicate and worth the effort. By the time the fire in the stove was reduced to embers, Marina and I were both bored and our conversation had become ingrown.

"His life is behind him?"

"His past."

"It says here his whole life is behind him, yet he is not dead. I'm quoting. His - whole - life - is - behind - him."

"You've done enough, Belka," said Larion in Russian, and the sudden change in languages shifted us from the world of academia back to the warmth of the dacha (*Belka*, little squirrel) as if a stage had rotated to place us in a new scene. Why hadn't his masculine authority surprised me? Maybe because Marina took it in such stride, even seemed to agree with it.

"That's all," she replied, in Russian. "We're finished for today." She smiled maternally and slapped the book shut, tossing it onto the bookshelf beside the divan. "Do you have enough blankets?" She sat on Larion's thighs and scratched his stomach.

"Yes. It's toast in here."

"Good. Then I'm going to bed. I'll see you in the morning, chipmunk," she said to me. She reminded me of the laundry lady at the dormitory, who had taken to calling all the Canadians her "little beavers." Marina locked herself in the bathroom and Larion walked into one of the bedrooms and began taking off his shirt by the light of a bedside lamp. There were only two bedrooms and the divan was clearly too short for me to sleep on.

"Where am I sleeping?"

"With me. It's a double bed." Buddies. Comrades: (Sp. *camaradas*) chamber-mates. There was nothing to his suggestion, but I felt my stomach contract as it had when my mind had fathomed the beauty of the porter's nape. That's been mentioned already, hasn't it?

When Marina came out of the bathroom, I hurried in. Masturbating would relax me, but my nervousness was too distracting. How could I concentrate when my pleasure had always been rooted in a respect without any specific location, had always hovered through my entire body or, more precisely, the bodies of others? I scrubbed my face and neck, brushed my teeth with the edge of my finger, and returned to the livingroom. Larion was waiting to use the bathroom and he passed by me without making eye contact, as if it was nothing more than a circadian ritual.

Under the covers, I curled into a fetal position, partly to hide my erection, partly to alleviate my childish anxiety. I scrunched up my toes, and counted them by sensation. I picked anxiously at my wart. It was frightening to think that my bed would soon be occupied by a man who was more often an apparition to me than an actual person. Was the gentle smell of sweat and soap his? Shall I worship it or is it somebody else's?

That word "man" back there frightens me. It makes it sound like I was sleeping with somebody in a business suit, a stranger. There are few people I would call men. This is not using the normative definition, or creating a new one really. It's just that "man" has always seemed like such an epic term, so large, so omnipotent and all-encompassing. But then, I can see the difference between "man" and "death." It must be that the term "man" has always suggested such status, but has never encompassed it. This is not a word game, or a political interlude. I'm actually trying to say something, and there seems to be no way out.

"You prefer the wall?" he asked, slipping off his pants. "So do I." White underwear that sagged under the gentle curve of his belly. Grey wool socks.

"You could have it if you want. I don't really care."

"That's fine."

My body lay stiff, hands curled under my chin, eyes directed toward the baseboard. It had not been his smell. He had the dirty smell of pepper and, when he raised his arm and tucked it under his head, of luxurious sweat. The winter wind hissed through a loose tile on the roof. It was warm now. My body began to relax.

"You have to excuse Marina's persistence. She's anxious to do well. Knowing English is opening doors." Was it his breath brushing against my forehead? It seemed he had moved closer to me. Should I curl toward the wall? Dogs do that, to avoid light. But if he was trying to say something, what reply would that action suggest but rejection? "Those translations must bore you."

"A little. I've never translated anything as complicated as this. Just word for word," I said in Russian.

"There's no such expression in our language. How is a word in one language supposed to constitute the importance of its underlying meaning in another?" In my pathetically desperate hopes (I see them as desperate now though they were almost unconscious at the time), I created a metaphor of underlying and lying under as in "We were lying under the covers; therefore, we were what was important." Something like that. Is that the blanket against my knee, or his thigh? These sorts of thoughts also getting tangled in the bedding.

"I hope it helps."

"I'm sure it does." All my senses struggled to feel the breaths of air that hovered over my eyelids. It was not sentimental of me to realize that those breaths were what sustained his physical beauty. The banner of those words "I'm sure" shut my eyes with their conviction. It was Larion's conviction that had made me worthy of his conviction. And then his arm, a banner of ownership and need, slipped over my body and I rolled onto my back so that the limb covered my chest. It was difficult to tell if he had realized what he had done. The warm darkness cradled us, wailing softly through the loose tiles on the roof until we fell asleep. Waking at one point in the night, I found us thoroughly entwined. My hand, a sublunar serpent, dared to wander over the slack slope of his belly to the soft mound of his cock, warm as goose eggs, and then I fell asleep once more.

The next morning, Marina, the servant, brought us tea in bed with rye bread and kiwi jam. It should have dawned on me then that it was not the new-found intimacy between Larion and me that she was celebrating. A storm had moved in during the night, dense white billows that jerked around the dacha-like oceanic waves, spitting cold through the cracks around the windows and doors. You could see the dry flakes, like letters from some untranslated alphabet, swirling against the glass. There was no question I would be spending another night. But rather than delighting in the opportunity the weather offered me, I feared the confinement that might eventually force me to admit my worship and risk the familiarity we had already attained. I seem to make my way to the edge of the abyss with great ambition but, upon arriving. . . .

Is it a fear that I won't be impressed, *eternally* impressed? Larion did not hurry to disentangle himself and I lay there, wide eyed, grinning like a dope, shrugging my shoulders lightly to suggest that there was nothing I could do besides wake him. Marina smiled like a stewardess and returned to the kitchen.

"Larion, it's 9 o'clock. Upsy daisy, don't be lazy. Time to go to schoolly-whoolly," she shouted and then walked back into the bedroom with more toast. Where had she learned those things? Some jargon text I imagine—*101 American Sayings for Daily Use*. She left the room again and there was the sound of more rye bread being dropped into the toaster. It seemed she intended us to spend the whole day in bed eating and translating Sartre. It seemed like such a friendly plan.

Friendship is not some degree between love and hate (what a fucked linearity these words suggest), but a sort of species on its own. It's like a Siamese fighting fish, attacking other fish regardless of their species. I did not want our relationship to mutate into friendship, for the social fungus would have clung to me until I died.

The three of us spent three hours laying in bed eating toast and drinking tea. Larion appreciated the morning's decadence more than his common-man attitude had suggested he would. In this embryo, Larion had become a person of this world rather than an emanation, a realistic process within my own existence. This bored me. At 12 Marina and I returned to the translations and by 3 we found we had actually read through most of the book. We ate an early dinner of scalloped potatoes, steamed cabbage, and kielbasa, and then Larion excused himself to take a nap. Marina did the dishes while I tidied the kitchen, the living room, and Marina's bedroom in preparation for her mother's arrival. Wandering through this three-room clover-leaf, I drifted from somnolence to malaise, entertaining myself with the image of a serf's languor. Neither Larion nor Marina seemed to notice my boredom. My reward was a sense of infinity. My sacrifice was time.

The windows showed stainless white, as if someone had snuck up during the night and covered them with coats of lime, and the rough winds continued to shout and whistle. The dacha was like the caves we used to build as children, from the snow father shovelled off the roof of the garage. The caves were connected to each other by tunnels and then, once we were inside, the holes were covered up lightly so that the 'enemy' would not know where exactly we were.

I can't remember what we did next but I do remember one particularly cold day in February that had killed chickens and frozen the dog's fur to the porch, when we were playing in the tunnels and I found myself passing from cave to cave without locating an exit to the open air. The freezing temperatures had quickly sealed all the vaults shut and my little boy body could not muster enough momentum in the cramped chambers to bust through. This seemingly unending chain of caves was actually a loop of only three caused by some malfunction in our architectural planning. Sobbing, I spun from chamber to chamber. My breath could not thaw the frozen snow; I became frantic but I didn't think to scream and then, finally, I fell asleep.

When my brother noticed my absence, mother made him bash all the icy bowers with a shovel. "If he broke your nose," mother screamed, "it serves you right. What the *hell* do you think you're trying to pull?" Nothing. Nothing was broken, but my lip and cheek were badly cut. The frozen tears under my eyes left marks like burns until the spring. My lip had become so swollen that I was unable to say Ps, Bs, labials in general, for days. Years later, my mother told me she had been so relieved to see me covered in blood because, from the steam, she knew that I was alive.

"But what if I was alive and he *hadn't* cut my face?"

"That would have been fine too, but this just made me so sure."

Me, sitting on the toilet while mother pressed cotton balls against my face, swearing and sobbing, band-aids clenched between her teeth. Her cigarette burning untouched, the ashes falling into the sink. And my sisters, from the other side of the bathroom door, jeering "Say 'Pied Piper'. Say 'Pied Piper'. Say 'Peter bought a peck . . .' "

"I have a question to ask of you which I do not know how to word." I was in the process of retrieving a coaster from under the divan when Marina said this, and grunted for her to continue. "Would you marry me? I would pay you, of course. And we would get divorced once we arrived in Canada." Her voice was stiff and practical, neither maudlin nor official.

"I don't know what you're talking about." I was standing facing her now, grappling with a situation that I could only think of responding to in platitudes.

"Would you please put your head behind the divan again? I cannot talk to you like this." Her expression was stern but her hands were shaking and her steely eyes flashed once at the open bedroom in which Larion was snoring. Finding the scenario uncomfortable myself, I complied.

"I have to leave this country. I have to." The sound of the bedroom door closing. "I love it here so much and it is going to kill me to leave." Her tone was amazingly steadfast. She was aware of the conflict and had recognized that it was unavoidable. Sacrifices had to be made. "Don't ask me why I have to do this. And why I'm leaving if it will kill me. That is none of your business but I have to pay the piper." At the time, I had wished that she'd chosen to speak in Russian, if only to avoid the clichés. The dust behind the divan made me sneeze but I did not change my position. A metal coil pushed uncomfortably against my right ear.

The images that Marina's suggestion conjured up in my
mind were of Larion and me living in the Rockies, gyres of
snow swirling like Catherine wheels about our cabin, both of
us young, chopping wood and stoking the fireplace, us in our
long, down-filled coats, swirling like the coat of the Pied Piper,
the incessant scent of cedar, our pale, strong hands, both of
us fifty, writing about the environment, the glacial ox-bows
of southern B.C., the mating habits of the carnivorous osprey,
sending our reports to a concerned government, both of us
old, writing, drinking coffee, chopping and burning cedar
trees that continuously sprung up not three metres from our
cabin, and then content, both of us dead and buried, laying
like knights beneath our long blue coats, beneath the snow,
like sailors buried at sea, but no. There was AIDS, Pied Piper
of Death. And guilt for this glorification of a mundane life.
At best, we will rent someone's summer house on Galiano for
a season. At best, we will unplug the phone. Or was this cabin
here in the Ukraine "at best"?

Marina was still talking, having switched from English to
Russian. "The situation is absurd, if you only knew, but I don't
want it to affect your decision. It is obvious I do not love you.
How could I? Don't make me say more than I have to. The
arrangements will not be a problem. I even know somebody
in Vancouver who will settle the divorce. Please put your head
back." The lunacy of the proposition overwhelmed me. I had
to lay on my back to continue breathing, my head still behind
the divan. Why had I not asked for reasons? What made it
sound like her needs and concerns where so grand that I
couldn't dare question her intentions? Though the answer
was "Yes." Most definitely "Yes." Here she was solving problems I had not even considered. Long term. Me, my own good
Samaritan. And all this time, Larion, snoring and wide-eyed
in the other room.

"The only hassle for you will be time. None of the arrangements will be your responsibility. And I will pay you." The

ragged snores coming from the bedroom echoed in my head. It was as if a single person was talking in her sleep, snoring and speaking. Larion grunted and the snoring stopped. Marina no longer spoke. And then I noticed that the congestive silence meant the storm had ceased as well.

"You can get your head out, silly. Can't you see I'm done?"

7

Larion was rustling noisily in bed. I know now that he had only been pretending to be waking up, that he had been listening all along. Marina was putting away dishes by the sink, her full arms flexing, relaxing, and re-flexing, like the pulse of waves. It seemed so alien, that domestic scenario, me crawling out from behind the divan, ensconced in my western aftershave. I went into the bathroom and washed the web of dust off my face. When I returned, Larion was sitting at the dining room table drinking tea and playing with a matrooshka, taking each wooden doll out of the belly of its mother and lining them all up along the edge of the table like a firing squad. A child from a child. Except that with a matrooshka, a doll could go missing and it made no difference to the structure of the rest. I am no longer a matrooshka. And then he put them all back together and invited me to walk to the lake. It was at that moment that I realized how complicit he was. Through petty friendship only though; the tenuous sublimity of our pure relationship proceeded without regard for Marina's manipulations. I still try to see it this way.

There are two narrators to any tale of distress, one within the other. Both inside each other. Only when it's laid out flat on the page like this does it appear linear. A topographical map of my emotion and my analysis of it. This is what the argument is all about. Structure becomes an allegory through which to perceive. Since the limits of this structure can be seen, there must be a format beyond it. Something without these constrictions, something as blank as a computer monitor. Or as blank as a screen blizzard on the television.

White with fog and scenery. A lake, quite large, frozen over
and surrounded by pine trees. A metallic sheet of fog waver-
ing over the ice, blurring the trees into flat, grey sentinels.
Every few hundred feet, a brick roasting pit constructed by
the government for the local citizens.

"Do you think you will marry her then?" He pushed the
words into the white silence between our mouths, as we swept
the snow off one of the pits with our sleeves to create a space
to sit down on. There was a plaque screwed to the masonry;
most of the words were covered in frost and rust but I could
make out "In recognition and remembrance of the following
men, who gave their. . . . " What? Who were they? Could they
be buried beneath the stones? Or maybe they just donated
the masonry: "In recognition and remembrance of the following men, who gave their bricks so that others might roast their
shashliki." We moved on to the next pit, to see if it was
dedicated to the same people.

"I guess this means we're melancholy," I said, recognizing
that a reference to our past suggested that I was already
constructing some sort of mutual history.

"I'm not, but I could understand if you are."

The next pit was dedicated to Laika, the first dog in space.
I looked it up in the Vancouver Public Library and apparently
the dog died up there. That wouldn't be so bad, finally
recognizing the space between yourself and the world. To
finally talk without everything falling into two dimensions.
But the Soviet scientists sent it up with no intention of
bringing it back down, disposing of the dog even while they
were still using it. There was no mention of this on the plaque,
just that it was the first dog in space and that it had helped
further the study of aeronautics.

It is much more pleasant to imagine a large, metal dog-
craft softly landing on the dog-pad to the shouts and applause
of a crowd of grey-suited dignitaries. The curved blue door
of the craft lifting as the crowd hushes and then, Laika, the

space dog, peering from the shadows, momentarily shy, unstable now on its earth legs, out of space, before marching down the dog-wide stairway to the podium trimmed with garlands and crepe-paper flowers made by some Pioneers from a nearby school. A wreath of ribbon and dog biscuits placed around Laika's neck. But this was not how it really was. No, it was cut off at the second stanza. "She went to the baker's to buy him some bread; But when she came back the poor dog was dead."

"I've never considered anything like this before. Is it done often? Is it complicated?" I hadn't answered Larion's question yet, their mutual question.

"I guess it's done occasionally, but we're not that familiar with the process ourselves. It's our first time also you know." He spoke as if I were to marry both of them. "She doesn't really *have* to leave. She wants to. She has her reasons."

"Did you want to go as well? Will my marrying her do anything for you?" If Marina's plan helped Larion leave the country then my marriage to Marina would be as much a marriage to him, and the image disconcerted me. It would mean placing constraints on him, adopting such a binding structure. I know what was typed in just a while back, what I have always been grappling with.

"If I have relatives in the States, it will make it easier for me to go. And I really must go."

"Why?"

"Well, I am homosexual. Nobody knows this. And two — I will soon have to serve my term in the army and I really am scared of that. I do not *want* to be but here we have it." Sitting on the roasting pit, feeling Laika's history getting imprinted on my ass, I felt, as Marina had said earlier, that it was none of my business.

"I do not expect you to understand," he continued, "but I am dead here. Neither a citizen, and I would love more than anything else to be one, nor something besides that, for there are only citizens here. They will not accept me, so I am a nonentity. There is no room for me." And in Canada? The fog had settled close to the ice and the pine trees shone as clear and green as jade flints in the distance. A paleolithic pastoral.

We proceeded over the lake, a quick-shifting, milky swirl of air struggling to gain enough energy to rise off the bed of ice. It coiled about our bodies like the robes of phantom saints. Gigantic, white worms, blind. Maybe just one. "I'll marry her. Why not? I'm not of this world anyway, if you only knew." Our arms were entwined, another thing buddies do in the Soviet Union without pretense. Pre-tense. Yes. Paleolithic. When we reached the other side I dared to kiss him on the cheek. His face was cold. "I'll help you too. I'm sure I can, once we're over there." It melted then into a smile and his moist lips pushed against mine. At the time I had thought the smile meant "Thank you" but maybe he had simply felt it appropriate. That he owed it to me. At that moment. Not always.

A crane appeared above the trees and sailed down toward the lake. "It's going to crash. Watch this. It's hilarious." Though we did not see the bird land because of the swirls of fog, we heard it touch down on the ice with a sharp thud. It rose from the mist about a hundred feet from where it had disappeared and then fell again. The bird stood once more and collapsed just as quickly. This spastic dance went on for a while and the bird's useless persistence began to aggravate me. Larion made his way toward the creature and, about twenty feet from the crane, he slipped into the fog as if he were descending a staircase, the way lifeboats sank on *Gilligan's Island*.

Soon after, the crane began to squawk desperately and Larion appeared from the mist, himself the image of some prehistoric, arctic bird, clutching the crane by its gangly legs, while the creature's silver wings spread and shut in smooth strokes like the blades of a jackknife. It must have had a wing span of over two meters. For a moment, as Larion rose on tiptoe, it seemed the crane might carry him off but then he released it and we watched the creature sail across the lake and over the jade pines, as sure as an arrow.

This all could have just as easily occurred here in British Columbia. The pine trees, the white ice, the bony crane dance. Larion, white within the white snow and silver sky, is the most real image that I have, *because* it is so Canadian in its space and limitlessness. The geography of the Ukraine is so like that of the Canadian prairies or the coast, so unnaturally beautiful. The almost urban clarity. It is not just the silver image of Larion which seems so comforting to me, but the open, infinite, perfectly monotonous space that that entire weekend represented. There was room for me there. There was room for Laika to land. There was so much room we didn't know what to do with it all. There was nothing but room.

Our seclusion in the dacha shadowed the seclusion of a womb, the three of us existing like one entity. As Larion and I lay sleeping, our breath would become syncopated, as interdependent and interwoven as our limbs. The first time I noticed this, I lay listening for some time before my own excitement threw my breathing off. The warmth he attained from sitting next to the fire would later that night become my warmth. The cool dampness of his hair would become my dampness. We had been consumed by the rhythmic beating of the milky blizzard just as everything else had, the village, the world, and all my conceptions of any other world. And when the storm lifted, the stainless haze remained in our eyes and in the endless terrain which surrounded us. Leave me this image. This snapshot.

Or leave me the image of Larion when he turned and faced me, grinning and waving his arms in imitation of the crane. I returned the gesture but felt foolish and old. Our hands fell to our sides and we stood staring at each other for a moment, naked on the crystal mist. He could not fade away. I could not lose him. Our mutual existence was the only possible one. A death for either of us was mutual because in the white fog on the white lake under the white sky, dichotomy no longer existed, nor negation, nor sin, nor crime. Nothing but room.

It seems to me that to commit a crime in this world is much like dying in both its immediacy and brevity, though criminals are more of this world than the dead. Only afterward, that is. They are alike only after the fact. Once criminals have completed a crime, they are no longer working against society anymore than the model citizens are. If you take your cigarette and butt it out, throwing the half-full pack into the dumpster, you are no longer a smoker. If you begin smoking again, you are a smoker once more. Once you stop stealing, you are immediately no longer a thief.

Larion and I spent the last half hour of daylight walking from roasting pit to roasting pit, reading the plaques. Most of them were dedicated to various war heroes, though some mentioned blue collar communists and super-achieving Pioneers. There was one dedicated to the first dog to survive a brain transplant. The dog, whose name was something like Velocity, or Verity, had its brain removed and replaced by that of a monkey. Its heart managed to keep pumping for twenty-seven hours with the monkey brain in use before something didn't click and Velocity died. The monkey, who was donated for the experiment by the nation of Ethiopia, may have had a name but, as the plaque was dedicated to the dog, it didn't matter. Immediately, no longer.

That winter I proceeded to make love with the mentality of a criminal, my crime being atoned immediately after the act. I came, I murdered, I committed no crime. Though even now I cannot be definite of my success, either with Larion or with Bogdon. I guess we could track them down and check.

Assuming my crime, that it was successful, how should society punish me for those ten seconds? And how does this measure in relation to my own death? And then, how does it measure in relation to everybody else's? Immediately, no longer, a point of zero silence is attained. The concern becomes ineffable. The text becomes futile. The text becomes, in my absence.

Larion and I and our fable relationship — the closest thing to two gay men living together in the Soviet Union that I have ever heard of. Though it was quite possibly going on all around us. Nobody else was aware of the thoroughness of our relationship. Thorough by conventional standards. Even more so by ours.

Thinking back, nobody would have noticed our devotion, everything seeming to have fallen so comfortably into place. Andrei covered for my absence at the dorm; he thought I was spending the time at Marina's, which was feasible since we were engaged. Andrei also looked after Motorhead, who had grown fatter over the winter and had a permanent blanche on his torn tail where the algae had been. Andrei had purchased a mate for the goldfish, though he never established the sex of either of them, and gave it the novel name of Tractor.

My infrequent appearances at the dormitory were further vindicated by the fact that Marina and I *had* become close friends. We spent most of our time in the third-floor library, where it was less crowded, translating French literature from English into Russian or from Ukrainian into English. Everybody was convinced we were in love. Could this mean then that we were?

If nobody had been told that I was gay, would that have changed anything? My childhood had been Canadiana—a basement bedroom with fake oak panelling and a dresser which my mother called "the chiffonnier" (as if each family only had one, as ours did), a double bed and a white cover with pom-pom trim in various pastel shades, a window big enough to crawl in and out of. My community included our barn, a grandmother, the smell of her. My friends and I went tubing down the river in the summer, skating along its edges in the winter. Community Bingo. Pussy willows along the tracks. Flattening pennies. Building rafts. Collecting crayfish and clams for the chickens. Digging the hotbeds. Skinny dipping and coon hunting. And messy pecks at sex. But no carwashes or basketball or live performances. A typical *rural* upbringing.

Marina and I attended live performances — symphonies and operas (which neither of us necessarily understood, as we sat in the back drinking from our thermos and snickering at the tacky costumes). How I had wished she were Larion then. *He* was writing his dissertation. *He* was preparing for capitalism. Marina had a particular fondness for performances at the organ hall (another strong Slavic building) just down the street from Gregory Maximovitch's church. The hall, which had once been a church itself, boasted dozens of archways barred with ratty ropes, dim rays of light sliding off the curvatures of the walls, blending into the ceiling's mindless caverns. The catacombs in the basement had been converted into coat-check rooms and all the penance cells were now toilets. Sections of stone murals had been removed and cigarette machines fitted in to look as if they had always been there. The two women in matching crepe dresses also seemed like they had always been there, sweeping the dusty basement tiles. So silent, they might have never even spoken to each other. They must have. Did they sneak into the women's can to share a cigarette and complain about the monotony of their job? To swear, under their raspy breath, at the unseen powers that be? To kiss and coddle each other's worn and lonely breasts?

The main floor of the organ hall was carpeted and stuffed with church pews. It was rare that Marina and I got a seat that allowed us a view of the pipe organ, squat and solid as a golden frog. A view was superfluous anyway, since the organ didn't move; no steam spewed forth from the sad, fluked jaws of the fat pipes. The organist sat in a pit that was hidden from the audience. Apparently the organ was so heavy that it sank a few centimeters every year and this was how the pit had developed. The rest of the church was also sinking, but somehow the architecture allowed the organ to sink independently. The entire city of Kiev, for that matter, is built on sand washed in from foreign lands by the Dniepr. It was difficult to imagine, listening to the sure notes of the organ spilling into the dark folds of the building, that everybody, the choir, the prim members of the KLK, their prim children, the organist, all of us, at that moment, were sinking into the dark, muddy depths of the river basin.

There is even a modern ballet called, I think, *The Sinking City*. It's hard to remember titles; there were so may different concerts. Is a faulty memory a sign of AIDS? I don't want to know. In Kiev, there seemed to be a ballet playing every night of the week, often two or three. Most of them were traditional: *Carmen, Eugene Onegin, Giselle*. Within five months we had seen four versions of *Swan Lake*, one version three times. We must have seen over a thousand swans in all, two thousand thin boned feet padding against the hard wood floor. And the black swan must have appeared at least a dozen times alone. Toward the end of this string of *Swan Lake*s, I began to fantasize about the black swan avenging herself. She was not, after all, inherently evil, was more a black sheep than a black villain. Sheep Lake. Social but non-societal. Any advertisement for the ballet that was slicked onto a telephone pole or the side of Gregory Maximovitch's church made me hope that maybe this version would let the black swan be the victor. Maybe all the female swans would be black. Or the ballet itself might take place in a lake of crude oil. That would work with the government's new environmental ethos. And when the new versions still had the same endings as the previous ones, I thought, maybe the dancer herself will become fed up. She must know what became of Leda. She did not have to be the eternal victim. And then there was a third option.

Marina and I always chose seats in back centre while the rest of the audience sat closer to the stage. During the early Friday shows the front rows of the hall would be lined with farmers, since it was the time between the closing of the markets and the train departures. The traditional urbanity of the ballet seemed lost to them, as they ate their meat tarts and drank their scentless, home-brewed vodka. Sacks and baskets of potatoes, turnips, and carrots lined the aisle-ways while rubber gloves, kerchiefs, and cutting knives lay at everyone's feet. The group of blue collars was always speckled with near-sighted professionals and, as one panned to the rear of the audience, the proportions inverted until, about two-thirds back, one's eyes settled on the quiet librarians and black-framed clerks, sucking almond roccas in the darkness and hoping for some witty variation to this week's presentation of *Romeo and Juliet*. It was the fusion of these diverse members of society through their appreciation for the art that was most relaxing, the melting of a political dichotomy made apparent by their territoriality.

At the time, it seemed that their indifference to my presence meant that I was also a part of the fusion, as was any other foreigner. But this was only shallow romanticism, for Marina and I had preferred to separate ourselves from the rest of the horde, sitting alone in the back, drinking our thermos of cappuccino and trying to converse in French. What might this have told me about Marina, her desire to separate herself, to speak French, had I been more observant?

Afterward, the two of us would go to the corner bistro for egg and mushroom pizzas and beer, and then start walking toward her flat on the other side of the city, though not far from Larion's. The metro was convenient but we preferred the stroll because the cold air made conversation difficult (one's face was kept buried in scarves) and we could enjoy each other's silent company and the rhythmic scraping of our boots against the icy stones.

An inaudible language developed from these strolls, consisting of changes in pace, nods of the head, vague hand gestures, and gentle brushes of elbows. It was a simple language of attention, sincere in its simplicity. Yet a power structure was clearly in play. The man set the pace, and the man put *his* arm over the woman's shoulder, though they were almost the same height, and she buried *her* face into *his* coat for warmth. The bias of our language might have passed unnoticed, except that I often imagined Marina to be her brother, treating her with fraternal affection, moist smiles registering in our eyes. It was not a conservative heterosexual image then, that we tried to present. During those moments, she became an equal process of my existence. At the steps of her flat, we would kiss good night through the layers of scarves, the confident push and release of our solid lips redefining the confidence of our friendship and the superiority the relationship had over the contrived subplot of our engagement.

Our first kiss had made me think of Larion, since only he had sexually excited me for so many months. I subverted this image by qualifying our kiss as a social convention. Later, simply the expectation prior to our kiss made me think of Larion, and then the silent conversations of our walks. By mid-winter, I was thinking anxiously of him from the moment we left the concert hall until I had returned to the flat and wrapped myself around his sinuous body, cast upon the bed like the sun-warped board of a shipwreck.

I began to think about Marina through his name. If we had plans to see a ballet, I might think, "Larion and I are seeing the Kirov perform *Yaroslav Moodrai* tonight," but not so consciously as all that. When with Marina socially, I was really with her brother. I almost typed "internally," that I was with her brother "internally." But that's imprecise. "Spiritually" makes me laugh, and "wholly" is more subtle, but the fact that I have to step outside of the image to define it as entire is too much of a sacrifice.

It's unclear, even now, whether Marina knew, at that point, that Larion and I had sex and shared his apartment as a couple. She knew I spent nights there but she probably had convinced herself that this was simply an arrangement of convenience, that Larion was making a sacrifice for the benefit of her freedom. As well as his own. Yet, when I renounced her suggestions to have sex, in my most moral tone (I having never had to be moral in the Russian language before), her own apathy suggested that she may have known I was fucking someone else. And who else could it have been? Or maybe she was fucking someone else and only suggested sex to me out of a sense of obligation.

I just asked her and she claims she wasn't fucking anybody. Not that I trust her. Not that she cares. As his sister, she probably knows that Larion is a homosexual. My younger sister did. Probably before *I* did. She and her girlfriends used to call me a "gaffer," saying it was British for "jolly, handsome fellow," like "dink" meant "well-dressed man." But she had made sure to point out to me earlier that, in the bathroom mirror, "gaffer" contained the word "fag."

"Interesting," I had said, turning other words up to the mirror while my insides melted once again, melted with fear. My mind searched desperately for someone to blame this gaffer-trait of mine on. Since my sister had pointed it out to me, I thought that she might have been its source as well. ("Stop being a pest. If it means jolly, handsome fellow, then why do you keep saying it to *him*." Thank you, mother.) But this was impossible; my sister was too common, too boring, far too concerned with her own competence. She was too unsure to create anything as peculiar as a homosexual. I must have been eight or nine when she brought this realization upon me. How could the social implications have made sense to me at such an early age? What world were they preparing me for? Why had they taught me this so soon?

8

Larion knew all about preparing for the outside world. He hadn't attended a single concert that winter because it was so important for him to complete his exegesis on *Sister Carrie* and get his degree. "How can I compete in a capitalist society when my social preparations are not on a par?" He was so excited to compete. And in a country like that, he probably got a better grip on the process in one season than he could have in a hundred Canadian lifetimes. I think his basic image of capitalism came from Dreiser. He was ready to shovel coal with a spatula in order to make money. He always said he despised Dreiser's "brainwash," his false sentimentality, and his romanticization of work conditions.

"But in Canada, his work is taught as a type of realism," I argued one Sunday morning, raising myself up on one arm and turning to admire his milky green skin. His greasy hair was shoved back off his face and roughly tucked under his head. I could still taste his cum in my mouth though I couldn't remember at what time during the night I had sucked him off. The Saturday morning rays were glowing like a monitor through the blinds, striping the room. The upraised, black arms of the chestnut trees paid a creaking homage to the thin gauze of cloud in the sky. Faint voices rose from the street below.

"Sure it's a realism. If there's more than one realism then it's obvious they aren't all real. Realism doesn't mean real."

"But that doesn't make them all false either. It's a matter of perspective. One person's realism is another person's . . . I can't think of the word." I rolled over onto my back and tried to recall the Russian equivalent of a word I could not remember in English. My mind was not into debating. I wanted toast and tea. I wanted toast and tea, and he wanted to compete.

"Yet you'd think if all these realisms were devoted to a unanimous ideal, that somehow they would be less diverse. Dreiser is obviously a naturalist, and even then, he's paid by some money-hungry capitalist." Larion was switching from English to Russian and back again within sentences, trying to make his argument as clear as possible.

"What's this about an ideal? Nobody's talking about ideals here. There won't ever be unanimous consent. How can there be if we all see differently?" I realized that the conversation was verging on pedantry. It was our version of the weekend crossword. Dueling pedants. Banners flew.

"The ultimate realism is the realism of the dominant order."

"The dominant order is always internal and individual."

"Society structures discourse and that is a conversion of the internal into the dominant order." Maybe if he had mastered contractions, his ideas wouldn't have scared me.

"Society only structures the official discourse. The internal needn't be communicated through external language."

"Internal language is based on external structure."

"Internal language has no structure because it's dynamic."

"Dynamics only exists in relation to structure, which is external."

"Internal meaning doesn't require language."

"Internal only exists in relation to external."

"Internal will only exist when external ceases to exist."

"Internal is death."

"Death is ultimate."

"Life is ultimate."

"Life only exists because of death."

"Death does not exist except when life ceases to exist."

"Death is inevitable."

"Death is void."

"Death is embryonic. Death is yonic!"

"And yes, life is phallic?" he giggled.

"You're anal retentive."

"*You* are the one that is anal retentive."

"You're dead," I laughed, covering his face with my pillow and pinning his arms down with my legs as I straddled his chest, a luminous green in the glowing days of winter. He struggled to free himself but my peasant thighs had him firmly locked.

"I am choking!"

"Then save your breath." I knew he wasn't serious because he wouldn't have spoken in English if he was. My erection was pressing against his chest and I slid it down his body until my torso covered his. He tried to wriggle out from under me but I had his legs pinned together and he couldn't get any leverage. I threw aside the pillow and began kissing his face, his neck, his collar bone. He lay motionless, eyes closed, not breathing. Silence = License. 'Please don't speak,' I thought, 'please don't.'

"I'm dead," he mumbled, clenching a grin.

"Uh-huh," I mumbled and continued to chew his ear.

I could feel the warmth of the sun on my shoulders as it burned through the morning haze. I had managed to spread Larion's legs apart and he was no longer struggling. He kept his eyes closed (he always did) and stayed limp while I fucked him. Afterward, he fell asleep and I realized that the bed sheets, which I had bleached only two days earlier, were dull peach in comparison to his glowing skin. The curve of his shoulder glittered with the sheen of my saliva like a frozen snowball in the sun, or a scoop of mint ice-cream. The gentle

curve of teethmarks. Later that day I told him he was green
and that I thought he was verging on magic realism.

"Green as a trout, right?" he said, leaning over the sink so
that the cantaloupe he was eating wouldn't drip on the floor.

"A trout?"

"Like 'The Trout Breaks the Ice.' Or at least that's the
green I always think of."

"What's that?"

"You haven't read it? *This* is magic." Taking a last bite out
of the cantaloupe, he threw the peel into the sink and ran his
hands along his pant legs. He went to the book shelf and took
out a slim, white volume. Hard cover.

"This is it, by Kuzmin. I think every homosexual in the
Soviet Union must own a copy, though officially it isn't being
published."

"How did you get hold of it?"

"I stole it from the library. Most of the books in there
never get touched. The librarians don't even know what they
have. I just sliced off the backing with a knife and walked out
with it. They won't miss it. Not that I care. It was covered in
dust when I got it. I had to cut the pages myself."

"How did you hear about it?"

"Oh they mention him when they teach pre-Revolution
poetry, *just* mention him. They prefer he sink into the unshad-
owed mire of the Acmeists. Besides the fact that he was gay,
and it's not that obvious, he's too apolitical for them."

Kuzmin wasn't the only author Larion and I read during
the second half of winter. We also read the complete essays
of Montaigne and, necessarily, Dreiser. It was also from these
three authors that the philosophy of our relationship arose,
or the one that I turn to in my more blissful moods. I think
now that, had it been some other three authors, the tragic
tone of my brief history would have been greatly altered. And
the tone of these words as well. Though I had already fucked
Larion without telling him I carried the plague, this point in

my life was the last opportunity for repentance. But had the authors been different, chances are I never would have fucked again. But this retrospection is simply a mental game. My history continued as perfectly as a pressed rose.

I could not appreciate the beauty of a fish's skin in relation to a repressed homosexual and some young, green-eyed boy, even if it was the colour of passion in medieval Russia. I probably knew this; I think it's the same in medieval English. And even though Kuzmin's green was truly beautiful (he refers to it at one point as a powdered emerald and, somewhere else, as the eye of a monkey), the poem itself is boring. But I told Larion I had enjoyed the piece and he brought out his copy of Kuzmin's novella *Wings*, which was worse. Again, the infatuation of an older gentleman, this one named Larion, with, in this case, a young student named Vanya. The older gentleman was simultaneously paternal, aggressive, obtuse and detached, and shifted in and out of Vanya's life, indirectly promising freedom and independence. Since it was I that was going to get us back to Canada (read freedom), Larion took to calling me Larion, which led to no confusion at all. I have attained a copy of *Wings* from the Vancouver Public Library and though, when Larion and I would read it together, we were able to plump up each paragraph with subtext, there's no denying its limitations now. This is the juicy part:

"Tomorrow I'm supposed to be going to Bari, but I could stay; it depends on you: if your answer is no, send me a note saying 'go'; if it's yes, then write 'stay.'"

"What do you mean, 'no' or 'yes?'" asked Vanya.

"Would you like me to spell it out for you?"

"No, don't, I understand."

When Larion and I read this text in the winter of 1986, 'no' and 'yes' did not refer to just love, or devotion, or commitment but also to the 'no' or 'yes' of existence. Both 'no' and 'yes' meant existence; the words were synonymous.

There was no option. Our translation had sliced off our tongues.

Larion and I would discuss our infatuation with particular paragraphs of the novella for days. We had rewritten the entire text until it fit us like a glove, like Saran wrap. Sometimes our attempts at defining the subtext ended in feeble conjectures. At other times, they would end with slogans we agreed summated the emotions Kuzmin was suppressing, for we were in full agreement on his psychological structure, though we were both amateur and disrespectful psychoanalysts. Still, at other times, we would whip the developing theorem into such a passionate tempest that the only possible banner was an equally passionate fuck. I understand now that these unarticulated consummations were the closest to the truth. The pedantry of the other efforts was nothing more than a use of time.

Our discussions of Dreiser were even less interesting. Larion would venture into Dreiser's political naïveté and I would sit back in awe at the complexity of my lover's political philosophies and the confidence with which he voiced them. While I had spent my years at elementary school memorizing the history of a royal family on another face of the earth and being asked to recite the planets in our solar system in order of their distance from the sun, Larion was being taught the basics of Marxist/Leninist philosophy. My ability to spew out a list of Egyptian pharaohs on command and build a log cabin out of popsicle sticks would have been countered with his administrative involvement in the Young Pioneers. And while I was crowning my successful highschool career with an A average and a post on the Stanley Humphries Senior Secondary team in the TV quiz show *Reach For The Top*, Larion was revamping the administrative structure of the Kiev Chapter of the Young Communist League (they might not be called Chapters) and writing essays on democracy in Panama and role hierarchies in the Kup P'low tribe of central Uganda.

(Yes, my wife says they are called Chapters.) My academic history left me with nothing but a milky skin of political knowledge, which any Young Pioneer could have punctured. When Larion finished his thesis paper in early March, I insisted we never discuss Dreiser again.

Montaigne was the only author of the three that had any great influence on our interdependent existence. Actually, it was probably Montaigne alone, and not the combination of the three, who led us to our ultimate actions for it was he who took our mute mutual worship and focussed it back on death. Until we began reading the essays, our worship was a private pleasure, a contained jewel we kept locked in our flat like a piece of pornography or a bomb.

I am not referring to our closeted relationship but to the possessiveness we had toward our affections. We were not prepared to realize the noncontext in which such purity existed. Hallowed ground. We thought we could possess our fusion, control it in some way, and it was through reading Russian translations of Montaigne that this new freedom was recognized. We realized that our pleasure had been rooted in a definition created by a social structure which did not include us. We had been carrying on a charade, like young boys inhaling the smell of tobacco on their father's mackinaw and imagining masculinity, like Gregory Maximovitch in his nocturnal garden of celestial communism.

And we realized that to develop a social structure for ourselves would be unrealistic. The only structure would have to contain the one we were raised in since to deny its existence would mean to deny our own. It is at this point in the philosophy that Larion's opinion and mine diverged. He felt that an individual could only accept responsibility for their own perception and also could only consider the structure of what they perceive, that there was no need to define more. But I, who had grown accustomed to death and had passed the same blessing given to me onto Larion, knew that total supplication to death would supercede the moral structures created for the protection of the ego, which is what Larion was unknowingly defending. After about ten minutes of discussion on this topic, Larion would shrug his shoulders and say, "It's only academic," and I would shrug mine and say, "It's only words," but really what I was thinking was "It's only life," and Larion would have agreed with me anyway but we would have been talking about two different things. I knew that if I remained patient, he would discover soon enough the plague within him and the microcosm of life which the existence of that guiltless germ contained.

Who am I trying to kid? Myself. My normalcy. My boring mediocrity. I know that there probably aren't many more months (when can I expect to begin dying?) and that, eventually, these months will get more and more difficult to maintain. Sick and dying time time time. This is all I have. I know now that the word for this dichotomous entity is AIDS. It has always been AIDS, even before the plague was recognized. It is this virus that guiltlessly devours, reaching its ultimate glory at the moment of its own destruction. You fucking stupid AIDS. Stupid stupid stupid fucking AIDS. I speak of death as an all consuming divinity, with no 'life and death,' and this is exactly what the AIDS virus is—a senseless, consistent, constant power which can bring all people, and therefore all their imaginings, to nullity. To zero silence. I should not have agreed to do this analysis at all. There is safety in narrative.

I am doing it again. I am going meta-mental. Who wrote that short story about the young man who has a fling in New York and then steps in front of a moving locomotive? I could have done that, sincerely, trains trains across the Ukraine, with a wheat shaft in my fist, rather than a rose. But instead I continued with my waning studies, or pretended I did anyway. The literature courses didn't interest me, since all we read were novels with titles like *How The Steel Was Tempered*,

The Steam of Our Engines, and *The Building of Turbine CV2.*
Participation in our required Physical Education class was so
poor that the instructor no longer attended, leaving the few
devoted students alone in a small auditorium with a ghetto
blaster and a Soviet aerobics tape that bore a conspicuously
military tone. I showed up once and that was enough.

In the last social geography class I went to (also required)
some time in March, the instructor presented the indifferent
cluster of students with a geographic comparison of the
Soviet Union and Canada. She had drawn a chart on the
blackboard which contrasted various facts about the two
countries.

USSR	CANADA
—largest nation in the world	—second largest
—largest supply of hydro-electric and nuclear energy in the world	—second largest supply of hydroelectric energy
—largest known resource of diamonds, copper, and gold	—largest known resource of tundra, peat moss, and bottled water
—first animal in space, first man in space	—built space arm for United States spacecraft

The facts continued on the blackboard to the instructor's
left, statistics about geography, demography, medicine,
knowledge, and numbers of time zones. This is something
else I checked, and Canada does have the largest resource of
peat moss, though, if it's any consolation, most of it is frozen
and inaccessible.

When the wedding date drew near, I stopped attending
classes altogether. The amalgamation of Marina and Larion
which had occurred within my mind during the winter was
no longer as apparent but when the time arrived to prepare
for the wedding I found myself still calling my fiancée by her
brother's name. She took this as a tolerable idiosyncracy and

eventually stopped trying to correct me. I was grateful afterward, though now I don't give a shit.

I toyed with the idea of Gregory Maximovitch conducting the wedding services, but since neither Larion nor I adhered to the religions of the churches, this part of the procedure was passed over. Instead, we were married at the official licensing bureau. The ceremony involved me and my fiancée signing administrative documents under the approving eyes of Lenin and an official dressed in a pink rayon dress and reeking of green onions. Only Larion, Marina, and I attended the signing and then we went to the Hotel MUP where my fiancée had rented two adjoining rooms for a supper of champagne, brie, and rye toast (in memory of our weekend at the dacha).

Larion and I celebrated our marriage with a quick fuck in the shower while his sister took a nap. The soap and precum on his loose foreskin were just barely enough lubricant; you know how if you concentrate, some of the sensation comes back. Afterward the three of us proceeded to get drunk, each for a different reason. I had never tasted caviar and demanded it, even though Larion claimed it was too bourgeois. It tasted a lot like semen actually, salty and slick. Bubbles of unfilling infinities, they were not worth marking a difference over. The taste on my teeth was Larion's, and I wouldn't force him to taste roe if he didn't want to. I wanted to lead him only to freedom, and never to limitation. I thought this then, but I was unaware of how double-edged a term like freedom was. Is. Can be. Much too big a word to be functional.

I just crossed it out of my dictionary.

I was nervous through the entire wedding and couldn't seem to get drunk. The marriage was more of a farce for me than for Larion's sister. I could neither act somber nor "make the best of things," as she suggested I do. After all, we were friends, the three of us, and it wasn't as if we were cowering in some freezing army bunker on the outskirts of Moscow. We had plenty of food, smooth booze, and a comfortable place to sleep. Almost anything would have been worse but I could not seem to enjoy myself; there was a chaperone in my wedding bed.

None of this mattered to my wife, who maintained a forced friendly demeanour throughout (how stereotypically Russian she must seem) even though the agitation caused by the day's abnormal proceedings showed clearly. Her eyes drooped and the skin around them was the colour of chicken meat close to the bone. When she spoke, it was in the clipped military tone of a bureaucratic functionary. I imagine things could not have been much more degrading for her. I wonder now, did she love one of us? Yes, her brother; they loved each other. And I never really thought about it until now. At the time, my only worry was that my wife might expect a fuck on her wedding night.

Because of AIDS and my new devotion, fucking for me was not a casual act. I could only have sex with those I worshipped, as aspects of the penultimate order, whether for their sublimity or, as with Larion, my union to them. I tried to merge my perceptions of Larion and his sister more thoroughly, in order to treat her with affection in bed, which is what I feared she expected, but when the contrivance of my efforts showed even to myself, I went into the washroom and stuck my finger down my throat until I puked, so that she would think I was drunk. After my third run, I returned to find the lights out and my wife motionless on her side of the bed.

"Don't insult me. What made you think I wanted to sleep with you?" She did not move her face from the pillow when she said this, her cursory tone trimmed with hostility.

"I thought you might want to. I didn't know."

"Well don't worry. Go to sleep." I sat on the edge of the bed, wearing the tight-fitting pajamas she had bought me. Was she worried that I slept in the nude, "like all Americans"?

How many times I had heard that there, "like all Americans," though, to be fair, I never heard it from Larion or Marina. I ate a chocolate, white and sugary. I could feel the grains of sugar as they tracked along the bumpy ridges of my tongue and then dissolved. Her sentences were always so final.

"I'm sorry for being so off today," I said. "The whole thing's become so screwed up. I don't know, maybe this wasn't a good idea. I feel like just dying."

"*You* feel like dying?" she hissed from under the covers. "*You* do?"

9

Though I never loved her, I considered killing her for her
sake anyway. With AIDS around, it's far less melodramatic. And since life with her was often so laborious, I thought
of doing us all the favour. She probably did know that Larion
and I slept together since, once we were married, she tried
everything possible to keep me from him. Except sleep with
me; that question never came up again until Canada. And of
course all I thought about was Larion, alone in his flat, waiting
for his defection, waiting for the freedom he already had but
which I could not tell him he had, because that would entail
my claiming responsibility for a process in which I was not an
authority but a vehicle. My worship/love/need of him, which
was already entire and therefore could not grow, took on a
shade of pity. It reads like mockery but there is such a large
dose of truth in all this.

My wife, in the meantime, ran about trying to "pick up
the slack" of our shallow marriage—canning tomatoes, hem-
ming curtains, opening bank accounts (there and in Canada).
Her idiotic, idiom-saturated logic grated against my tired
senses. Sometimes I got her to write the sayings down for me,
and I still couldn't understand their meaning. "Leaving your
tail in the trap," for example. Or (she offered this one today)
"Mending London's crack." And they seem to become more
convoluted the longer she speaks the language.

She quickly transformed our sloppy, grey flat into an
urban dacha, with thick rugs on the floor, a tapestry of Acteon
over the crack on the wall, and tacky Turkish ceramics on any
unused shelf space. The windows were kept clean and frilled

and, out on the balcony, the cabinet which served as a fridge was always so stuffed with fresh borscht and *nalesniki* that there was no room for milk and I had to go out every morning (upsy daisy, don't be lazy) to the dairy store to pick some up. My dormitory possessions were packed into boxes, transferred to our flat, and shoved unceremoniously under the bed. I let Andrei keep Motorhead since he claimed that, even though Motorhead had eaten Tractor's eggs, the fish were in love. It turned out that Gregory Maximovitch had transferred to a better paying job in Odessa. The new priest was younger and physically more attractive than Gregory Maximovitch, with stringy white hair that he kept smoothing over his bald spot. He had the nose of a collie, the nostrils arching in such a way so as to expose almost half of his nasal passages and the strong, white hairs which filtered them. My father has the same nose. Maybe I would have had it as well.

I tried befriending him, but he could not understand that I didn't need anything from him, that I simply wanted to smoke in his basement and talk. He was deaf in one ear and his name was Bogdon Nebavovitch Bezglasnov. I had come across it yesterday while digging through my Soviet Union paraphernalia in preparation for today's typing. I had written it down because it was a name I knew I would never remember. If somebody had rifled through these scraps of paper after my death, this is the name they would have come across, the only name—Bogdon Nebavovitch Bezglasnov. Not Larion, nor Gregory, nor Paul, not even *my* name, but this one, Bogdon. And his church. Maybe my mention of this new priest will be edited out. "He does not contribute sufficient information." Should I say he is a theosophist, to complicate matters? A devil worshipper? Should I say he walks as if stepping on lilies not yet blossomed? On lotus petals? Silent as white noise. The winter of white noise. And the number one question of the season: Who decides who belongs in whose history?

When Larion was sent to the country for three weeks to help with spring planting, Bogdon Nebavovitch's church was my only hope of an outlet. But after two stilted chats on the state of religion in the Soviet Union, I avoided the priest like my wife, sneaking into the church basement and smoking for hours alone in the darkness. Not even moths or the electric glisten of a drip of water. Not even the light bulb any longer. Larion's absence actually made my marital confinement more tolerable, since his own isolation was not nagging on my mind. And I hoped that maybe the brisk country weather would speed up his deterioration. Often, while walking the streets so as to avoid the domesticity awaiting me each night, I would find myself in front of his apartment building, gazing at his flat like one of the uninvited. Though I had a key, I didn't want to enter that chamber of tactile mementoes which could not even symbolize our devotion. Nothing could and, though I had been handling his absence well, the limitless void it created soon caught up to me. Let it be over with, I thought. Then I'd go and eat at some restaurant and return to my flat when it was time to go to bed. Sleep was my only solace, wet white against the white sky and white mist on the ice, and I revelled in the innocence of voyeurism. I finally admired him from a distance once again and, though realizing that the indulgence belittled the divinity of our bond, I allowed myself the consolation in anticipation of his return.

Regardless of this blissful sleep, I woke each morning tired and apathetic. My skin was waxy and bloodless. The university sent generic letters questioning my absence. My wife paid no attention to my health, booking our flights to Canada and making several trips to the dacha for the possessions she intended to take with her. I sold my winter clothes on the black market so that she could afford to ship all her luggage. She took the train to Moscow weekly to visit her mother and establish the codes they would use to arrange Larion's defection. I did not want to meet the mother. I became hostile toward my wife, even when she wasn't around. This wasn't degeneration; the symptoms occurred almost simultaneously.

And somehow, amongst all this, I found myself admiring the physical beauty of other men once again (the little girl in Poltergeist: "It's back!"), rediscovering the undulation of tendons on the back of a broad hand, the two-fold ripple of the muscle between the ankle and the calf. Like something out of Kahlil Gibran: "Open yourself to the answer and it will come to you." But I knew that in the Soviet Union, you had to sniff it out yourself. I found myself scouring the dry, barren forests of Hero City Park once more. Hours were spent sitting on slushy benches watching young children cross-country ski and old men, bent from the weight of their medals, plod along the paths. Until I became ill and my excursions to the Lake of Fags stopped.

My nose ran incessantly and a scratching dryness crept into my throat, waning only when I went to sleep. Even climbing staircases became a chore and so I began spending all my time mopping my nose and waiting for Larion's return. My wife made herbal balms for my nose, and berry teas for my throat. She pinned a wool sock around my neck with a safety pin and laughed in my face. She gave me garlic cloves boiled in milk to eat every night before going to sleep. It was clear to me that I might die without seeing Larion again and I began studying Montaigne religiously, reading Book II for entertainment and the first twenty essays of Book I, over and over again, for a sense of wholeness. "By diverse means we arrive at the same end." The date of his return arrived and I was still within this reality. But unfortunately bed-ridden. Or was it fortunate? Did it circumvent my use of language in trying to explain how I was dying without him? But then, isn't illness also discourse?

Marina met him at the train station and brought him to the flat, where I had spent the last week in bed. When Larion

saw my condition he fell upon my chest and cried, which
surprised my wife, because she had never really noticed the
extent of my deterioration until then, and saddened me,
because I had been carrying the hope that my sickness would
be the catalyst which would make him realize our fusion was
a fusion within the sphere of death. I was so tired of carrying
on. Every effort at comprehension seemed to have led me
back to a sense of my own mediocrity.

"He's thrown the basin on the bricks," said my wife, to
Larion, shaking her head. "I've tried everything but he won't
get out of bed."

"I can't," I said, though I was already sitting up and just
waiting for Larion to signal our departure.

"Can you stand? Try." And I did, much to my wife's
justified agitation. She snatched the bedding off the bed as if
it were sprinkled with lice, and stuffed it into the laundry bag
which sat on top of the wardrobe. "I feel a bit woozy, but I
can walk just fine." I didn't care if my wife saw me as a
hypocrite. I wasn't sure whether I should be strong, so that
Larion would be proud of me, or weak, so that he would take
me home. Double time. I was there and I was not quite there.
Near. Wrapped in Saran Wrap. Participating yet objectified.

I moved back in with Larion without a concern for my
wife's desire to depict social conformity. I was so sure it was
AIDS time this time. Larion fed me bullion and kielbasa,
crooning, "Drink this. We need you," and smiling wryly. I had
forgotten, I was his salvation. So now, as I type this, I'm not
sure whether my health improved because of Larion's concern for me or mine for him.

There were only two months left before my departure and
I was now anxious to arrange Larion's defection, on my terms.
The channels my wife had chosen suggested a minimum of
eighteen months before he would arrive in Canada, and I
wanted him there sooner. Through the Canadian Consulate
in Moscow I learned that he could get a one year visitor's pass

within three months of his sister's arrival in Canada if all the necessary documentation was filled out before our departure, but when I presented this information to Larion, he was hesitant. We were sitting together on the couch watching Soviet news, drinking beer, and eating waffles. The announcer was talking about Vancouver, as it prepared for Expo '86. "Sister city to Odessa, clean, with fresh air and much greenery," and film footage of families in Queen Elizabeth Park, shoppers on Granville Island, homosexuals promenading along the Fruit Loop. Vancouver seemed clean in my mind then, scrubbed and bleached in my absence, and these images had to have pleased him as well. This was the point all along.

"I do not know if I could go that quickly," he said, scratching a small wart on his left index finger. He stared at the sink with an abstract expression on his face. "I have to organize things here. And ensure that mother is set up and doesn't need me. I'd like to know the results of my final year at the institute since it would help me compete in Canada. We don't have the money for a third ticket and I don't want to go as your dependent." Now the television was showing models of False Creek as an Expo site, the bubble of B.C. Place surrounded by glass warehouses. "My aunt in Tbilisi just got approval for the construction of an addition to her home and, since Boris has gout, she has asked me to help her build it." Neither of us took a breath during this recital. Bubbles bursting. Glass houses pelted with stones. I hit him on the head with a throw pillow, a wedding gift from the laundry lady at the dormitory, and laughed. But he was silent. And then it didn't matter, whether he was serious or not.

"Listen. Listen."

The television announcer was speaking in an anxious though controlled voice. The footage of Vancouver had been replaced with a map of the Ukraine, cream coloured with a black dot just north of Kiev. He was telling us that the nuclear accident was contained. That the flames had been extinguished and no further gas was being emitted. All the workers, he said, had been evacuated. Two people had died and nobody was injured. I could hear the squeals of young girls playing on the sidewalk outside. "Ladybug, ladybug, fly away home," they sang. I could hear the steady thwack-thwack of their skipping rope against the concrete.

It didn't take Larion's sister more than five minutes to arrive at our house, dragging two suitcases, her chest heaving under her thick, grey coat. Her hair was scattered in chunks on her head, like a cheap wig.

"What's wrong with you two? Don't you answer your phone? What are you doing? I've been trying to get train tickets all fucking day. I have two to Moscow and one to Ryga." She shoved the tickets at our blank faces with her mittened hand. I was irritated by her sensational entrance. "What? Didn't you hear yet? There's been a nuclear accident at Chernobyl. Pick tickets. I don't care which one I get."

"Is *that* where it happened?" asked Larion. I was mesmerized by the knitted pattern on the mitten she had dropped. I didn't need this intrusion, this new force. Blue reindeer, or caribou maybe, marching an infinite loop around her wrist on a blood red sheet of ice that extended to her fingertips. She walked anxiously to the window and looked out, like Dorothy's auntie checking for the twister.

"Yes. They're bussing the villagers into Kiev. We have to go to Moscow. Better I take the Ryga ticket. I'll find my way to Moscow easier than either of you slugs. Help me get the rest of my luggage. And try to call a taxi! I can't reach a taxi. And mother too. Call mother. Your train leaves in an hour."

"But the announcer said it was contained. That there was nothing to worry about." My tone was casual, cocky maybe. By this time I was recalling my superior position.

"How the fuck does he know!" she shouted back at me, already at the bottom of the stairs. Alla crooned to a ship with a Finnish name, "Bye bye my sailor, the current spins around," while we waited for my wife's return. The line to the taxi station (1114-4434) remained busy. We also turned the radio to BBC to hear the western reports. It was at this point that I fully comprehended the fickleness of death. With one segment of a squeak, the radio announcer had offered us freedom, a personal, divine reward beyond the bureaucracy and illogical demands of nations. I am not sure exactly how I realized that a nuclear accident was a release as much as a confinement, that we were being offered immortality while, as far as I knew, our insides were melting like the cherry syrup in a Hallowe'en candy skeleton. It was a new freedom in every way. Two homosexuals disappearing amidst the apocalyptic destruction of "Soviet bungling" (as the British radio station called it). Larion's list of excuses were nothing but fall-out, and the obvious possibility of our death meant he had to be on the verge of accepting my view. This meltdown, for one brief scandalous moment (a moment no longer than a day perhaps) allowed all of us to feel no guilt for individual perception, for telling society to fuck off and die for a moment, for a day. Our mouths melted open.

But while I revelled in the anarchy of disaster, Larion had turned clammy and began to sweat heavily. The pale, long hand holding his toast and jam shook so violently the food crumbled and scattered onto the couch. He did not ask if we were in danger or if there was something we should or could do. Obviously nobody knew and the Soviet television announcer who had now replaced Alla kept repeating that everything was under control and the government knew exactly what to do. Might this have been all that was written on the sheets of paper in front of him? Was he in the process of realizing his own freedom, there on national television? When all concepts of control are removed, the fear of anarchy might also be erased.

As the catastrophe led me into freedom, blissful anarchy, an atonement of my sins as well as a white-wash of social determinism, Larion (who still did not see death, did not see it as a favoured post) fell further into social responsibility. He began trying to phone his mother every thirty seconds and packaging various belongings into plastic bags for shipping, a useless process since all the post offices were clogged within hours of the broadcast. When he realized this, he stopped and began wrapping all our food in aluminum foil.

Marina arrived with the rest of her possessions including, for some reason, a broom and an end table with the price tag still attached. Maybe because they had never been used. Maybe she had intended to take them to Canada with her. "Did you get a taxi? Don't worry about mother. She knows enough."

"I don't think the phone is working," said Larion, though we hadn't called the taxi station in the last half hour. "I'm not going today anyway. There's no reason to doubt what we hear. You're panicking. Between you and the radio announcer, who do you really think knows more?"

"You're stupid. You think they'll let us into Canada if they find out we were in Kiev when Chernobyl blew up? Don't be so stupid, Larion." She was dialing the taxi station in a state of terror, cranking the dial hard as if this would give her a better chance of connecting.

"I'm not going either. We won't reach a taxi. We won't get on that train whether we have tickets or not. And there's no reason to panic. This is a nuclear leak we're talking about; what's happened, has happened." I called it a leak but hoped for nothing short of armageddon.

"*You* can talk. They'll take you back on golden horses, to check the biological effects of radiation. But there's no way either Larion or I are leaving this country if they find out we were in Kiev when it happened."

"But maybe our radiation levels are dangerous to Canadians?"

She ignored him, dialing again.

"Go to Moscow. I'll stay here with Larion to see what's happened. You'll be able to leave because you're married to me. And if you can convince Larion to go, great, but otherwise he's staying anyway." This summation appeased my wife who told me to continue calling a taxi and to mail her luggage before I came to Moscow.

"This is truly amazing, if you think about it," she said. "The entire world is dying. A goldfish is dying as quickly as a giraffe. A plum, as proudly as a grandmother. It really makes no sense at all. Or maybe this is perfect sense. Everything melting together." She stood like one of those dazed characters in Tolstoy's sagas, like Anna Karenina falling on her knees before the train and then asking herself, "What am I doing? Where am I? Why?" She seemed to realize that the speed of her departure was not a major determinant of her health, the facts being so vague. She gathered up her purse, jacket, and red mittens without looking down. "I guess I'll see you soon." She pecked my cheek, hugged Larion, and walked slowly down the spiral stairs, as if hoping we would call her back.

The accident occurred on a Saturday and so we had to spend the entire weekend in our flat to avoid potential fall-out. It was like that weekend in the dacha with its isolation but, even though Larion's sister was not there to irritate us, neither of us really enjoyed those days. On Sunday morning, the meteorologists on the television told us that the radiation cloud had travelled northwest into Poland. On Sunday afternoon they told us the cloud had passed 120 kilometres north of Kiev and was now in the south Urals and expected to rain. On Monday morning the cloud was still gravid and somewhere over the Mediterranean . . . .

They also told us not to worry about fall-out but that, if we *were* worried, showering twice a day and leaving our shoes outside should appease us. Larion and I followed these instructions. The announcer also recommended a wide brimmed hat but, since we did not have any and the local univermag was sold out, we took the risk. It all seems so daft to me now. Our actions were like a mockery of the accident itself, pretending that a bonnet and a bottle of Sputnik shampoo would somehow protect us from fall-out. I was so impatient for Larion to realize, to realize. On Sunday night, the British radio station reported that the city of Kiev had been flattened and that the foul Dniepr was in the process of contaminating the entire Mediterranean. We had a good laugh; things were lightening up.

On Monday morning Larion wanted to go to the university to ensure the administration that his absence was temporary. We stopped at his sister's flat to see if anyone had been by with messages. There was an envelope with the insignia of the Canadian Consulate tacked to the door and a box covered with an army blanket at our feet.

On top of the box was a note from a student at the institute, and inside the container was a bounty of food. The note said that she, the student, had returned to her village in northern Moldavia where "Father Wisdom insures me that life will be safer and cleaner," and that the food had been sent to her by some relatives from home and was therefore radiation free but that, since she was leaving, she could not use it. The basket contained a bag of flour, a jar of sugar, two tins of sweet cream, cantaloupes, apples, two unskinned rabbits, two jars of pickled eggs, jams, tea bags, powdered milk, oregano, pepper, a book of Georgian recipes, and the latest issue of *Pravda*, each article individually wrapped in aluminum foil. We took the note, the pickled eggs, rabbits, and sugar, and left the remaining food uncovered to tempt the neighbours.

Bakeries, milk stores, and grocery stores were open though basically empty. Endless line-ups dangled like entrails from the post offices, ticket stations, and bus stops. We flagged a cab. At one point we passed a person standing in the middle of the highway wearing what appeared to be an apiarist's outfit, panning the air with a bulky instrument resembling a Weed-eater. The cabby wasn't sure whether this had anything to do with Chernobyl.

The university was almost deserted. Instructors sat by their stacks of reference books in front of classes containing only one or two students, none of whom were foreign. A banner, advertising a lunchtime celebration of governmental efficiency in mobilization procedures for the Chernobyl accident, hung in the main lobby. When we reached the administrative office, it was closed. A friend of Larion's told a nuclear joke. I don't remember it exactly but it had something to do with a fluorescent light bulb and Chicken Kiev.

We decided to go to the hospital for a radiation check, since the television announcer had suggested that those people who were concerned do so (though there was nothing to be concerned about). The makeshift waiting rooms set up for those waiting to get into the actual waiting room were packed, but when we informed the nurse of my foreign status, we were let into the waiting room. Among the crowd was Bogdon Nebavovitch Bezglasnov. The room was divided into two sections and at first I thought it was professionals and workers, which amazed me, but then Bogdon Nebavovitch informed me that the people at the other end of the room were farmers from villages near the site. The nurses and doctors dealing with them wore rubber gloves and paper face masks. The villagers were all huddled into a corner, like Christmas carollers, and they all wore red numbered tags over their hearts.

"They just check if they glow in the dark," chuckled Bogdon Nebavovitch. Having positioned himself so near to God, he was not concerned. Gregory Maximovitch had called and asked Bogdon Nebavovitch to join him in Odessa until the commotion had died down. The priest was excited about the trip; it would be his first holiday in over twenty years. I was mesmerized by a string of snot which clung to the inside wall of his left nostril. Both Larion and I showed innocuous levels of radiation on our heads and thyroids, though Larion did have a small infection in one of his glands which they told him to have checked if it did not go away within a few months. The radiation on my sneakers was above average and I was instructed to wash them and my socks in bleach. We stopped for lunch at the café where Marina and I used to have pizza. A long-haired waitress with a seductive lisp ensured us that the eggs had been shipped up that day from Zaparozhia. The disrespect of the citizens for their nation had been making Larion more and more belligerent all day. He began reprimanding the waitress for her cockiness, and she fled through the swinging doors into the kitchen. We ate our pizza in silence, watching the occasional citizen pass on the sidewalk. The air was brisk. There was not a cloud in the sky.

The prices in the open market had risen overnight, all the peasants claiming that their vegetables were planted the furthest from the nuclear plant. One woman even guaranteed us that her potatoes were shipped in from France. Larion refused to pay the raised prices and we returned home with nothing to eat but pickled eggs and rabbit.

While Larion laid the rabbits on a piece of newspaper and began to skin them, I opened the letter from the consulate, which I knew would be a request for me to leave the city. The British radio station, whose lines the Soviets chose not to jam for some reason (maybe they couldn't), had already reported that all Commonwealth students had left the country and that the only foreign students still intending to remain in Kiev were from Finland, Ethiopia, Cuba, and Costa Rica. None of these countries, the British station pointed out, had nuclear plants of their own. The station also claimed to have received reports that hospitals were being flooded with children who had holes burned through their abdomens and urinary tracts from drinking the milk of cows which grazed near Chernobyl. When I turned on the television, the Soviet announcer was reporting that the fire definitely had been contained and engineers were in the process of capping the plant to suffocate the flames. Furthermore, the incident had provided Soviet scientists with nuclear information that would place them well in advance of any other nation in nuclear technology and safety. Yippee.

The sound of fur being torn from flesh is still precise in my mind, I guess because I'd never heard it before. And the fact that there was no blood. Larion by the sink, wearing my army pants, holding that sandy sheet of fur in his fist. I went into the bedroom so that he wouldn't distract me. The letter in the consulate envelope was hand written by a man stationed in Hotel MUP to help the Canadians leave. He had train tickets for all of the Canadians and he couldn't understand why I had not contacted him. The note informed me that, though no other Canadian students had yet asked for tickets to leave Kiev, they all intended to. That evening, we had a wonderful dinner of roast rabbit.

Now the radio and television were turned off only when we went to bed. We spent the week reading Montaigne and eating rabbit stew and radiation-free pancakes. Our feelings reached out beyond us. The room had become stifling and my relationship with Larion had lost its spontaneity. Both of us were suffering from ennui. The contradicting news reports quickly lost their entertainment value. We no longer had sex. Since fucking had become synonymous with death for me, the nuclear event had filled me with reverence and my own endeavors seemed petty and worthless. Larion was depressed and distant, though I was confident our fusion, though less vibrant, did not waver.

I called the consul and told him that I was not prepared

to leave. When he asked where I could be contacted, I gave him the number at my wife's flat and he told me that that number had been disconnected. I told him I was at a phone booth and would contact him later with another number. He then told me he was having trouble attaining train tickets because he did not speak Russian and was wondering if I knew where the consulate of any Spanish-speaking nation was.

I was prepared to leave Kiev. There was no reason for us to stay and my plane's departure date was approaching. I brought up the subject while we were bleaching our socks in the bathtub. It was then that Larion told me he had decided days earlier that he would not be leaving the Soviet Union. I am not sure whether I had an inkling but wouldn't admit it to myself; what difference does that make if I hadn't acted on it? When I began to argue, he said I was being selfish.

"It's not selfish to want to remain with you until we die."

"It's selfish of you to expect me to leave my country when it needs me most."

"What can you do for it now? Either this accident is nothing or it's everything," I argued in Russian, throwing the sock I had been scrubbing into the water and standing up. The sky had been clear for days, and a crisp spring sun jabbed around the edges of the window.

"Or it is something," he snapped back in English. "I was taught to think of this country as my mother, a hard, disciplining but nurturing mother. Imagine that your mother is sick, that she is slowly dying of some incurable disease or suffering for a long, painful time. When she is healthy and things are going well, she gives you everything you need and, if she can, more. She gives you food and clothes and teaches you and just basically looks after you. When she is sick, what are you going to do? Let her die alone, because you do not need her anymore? Because she cannot give you everything you want?" He was on his knees, looking at the dingy water and scrubbing his sock-covered hands together vigorously as if they were stinging from frostbite. He reminded me of a photograph I had seen once of an Old Believer genuflecting in High River, Alberta.

"Do you really think you can give me everything I want, that you're some kind of Larion?" He had tears along the bottom rims of his eyes. His transparent hair lay over his forehead like onion skin. His lips glistened, and twisted as they shook.

"It's you who named me that!"

"It's selfish of you to think that." He switched into English. "It is selfish of you to think that somehow you will give me more than this country has. You see the assholes out there, laughing at her. But when they need some food, or a place to stick their fucking kids, who do you think they turn to? What do I need? Intimacy and a good fuck?" He was screaming at me through sobs now. He had stopped rubbing his hands together though they were still encased. Some sort of grotesque puppet show.

My mind could not pay attention. It could not step back and analyze. All I kept thinking was that I had to teach him another obscenity besides "fuck." I was trying to trivialize an issue which demanded my participation. He was looking into the tub again, or maybe his eyes were closed; in my memory, I cannot see his face. He was on his knees, facing the soapy water, head bent down, but I cannot see his face. I wanted him to know his own death so much it twisted my stomach and I had to pee furiously. Paul has told me that many AIDS patients lose control of their bowels as their bodies disassociate. The body leaves but the soul remains to mourn, an inverted death. We pee at the most serious moments in our lives. Everybody, everybody, urinates upon death. My final wish—to locate death and piss on it. A final atonement, absolution. A washing away of sin.

"I'm sorry," he said over the sound of my splashing piss, the knot in my bowels loosening, "I didn't mean to say that's all you've given me. I'll die without you. What else is there to do? That's almost incidental now though, now that this has happened. At the hospital today, I was even hoping they'd find I had radiation poisoning just so I would have no choice but to stay, just so I wouldn't have to go through this very argument. If Canada is so wonderful, stay here. There's something here for you to do. What's the rush?"

"I can't stay here. They won't let me. And that doesn't matter. 'Where' doesn't matter." And now here I sit, weeping before my Packard Bell.

10

My decision to leave had not surprised Larion. He said he knew I would not stay because my lack of political concern would not permit me to comprehend his scale of devotion. This was after we had stopped crying, drank a bottle of vodka, fucked, and were recuperating on the sofa. I had never heard anybody speak tenderly about political conviction before. He made it sound like a relative or a sick cat that had crawled under the porch to die. And catty too, he was sounding catty.

Maybe I went about it all wrong. Maybe we had been as much a unit as I had imagined, and it was our languages that were not interchangeable. I began this text with an attitude that I still hold; after all, how much can change in one long day? I guess an entire history can change, if it is recorded in that day. There is an irritating sense that I have undercut myself, and continue to do so, for even though the secular world will give me nothing, not even a blushing image, no matter how sincerely I ask, I continue asking. How, though I ignore it, does this hope manage to remain within me? What has the keying of this information into my computer actually succeeded in doing? It has allowed me to slide off of the origin of my impetus. Or, rather, forced me to separate myself from it. What else can that glowing thing on the screen be? My motivation has multiplied — changed and spread into this other program. But has this led me any closer to explaining my history? To anybody? Maybe I should have begun this memoir further back in time, before being tested positive, to clarify the origins of these seeds. Or before I met

Paul. Or before I was eight, inverting words in the bathroom mirror. I am tired, tired of the devotion in this text; I want to be absolved, so that I can rest. This does not seem to be who I am either. In the back of my mind runs the notion that perhaps my love for Larion was as escapist as my relationships with the Leonids or with Gregory Maximovitch. But it is a blind notion, blind in that I really cannot imagine it. I try to picture us, Larion and me, standing on a street corner, or in a warm kitchen, or in a barn surrounded by wholesome cattle, and me having this taking-a-shot view of him, but the image doesn't hold. It doesn't even form. No symbols of our devotion have developed beyond our pithy skulls. What a relief this realization is. This is the point of origin.

There must be something cathartic in the confidence of cows. The Ukrainians seem to love them more than any other domestic animal. At the univermag one can buy bovine versions of anything — cups, creamers, garbage cans, gaiters. On the day I left Kiev, the British radio station reported that all the cows in the north central Ukraine had died from nuclear radiation, and this had upset Larion greatly. The announcer had also stated that traces were being found in cattle in Poland and reindeer in Finland. High levels of radiation were also found in the tomatoes of southern France and the cocoa crops of Burkina Faso. The United Nations was preparing an official reprimand to the Soviet Union for not reporting the accident sooner. The Soviet reply was complete but they were waiting first to be officially reprimanded.

The announcer went on to say that children were not yet being allowed back into Kiev and that citizens of the city were still substituting apple juice or beer for water while tests on the Dniepr, which passed Chernobyl upstream of Kiev, were carried out. And that new cows were being shipped in, as well as truck loads of untainted, Siberian grass.

The Soviet television announcer, who had become as familiar an image as Alla, ensured me that there was no further worry of nuclear fall-out, and that the cloud had fully dissipated somewhere in the North Atlantic. It was believed that the United States had sent toxic fumes into the cloud as it passed over that nation in an attempt to alter the true intensity of the radiation the cloud carried. The final fall-out may have affected a small community of Arctic penguins but the animals were being monitored and no negative side-effects had yet been noted. Stay tuned for further updates.

Then a female announcer came on to say that the Soviet and American scientists were working in cooperation to put out the last of the flames at the site of the Chernobyl incident and that regular bus schedules to the area would soon be reinstated, though it was recommended that curious citizens remain out of the area until the plant was functioning normally once again. She added that, since Kiev's water was supplied by wells located in the mountains near the city, the rumours of water contamination caused by fall-out in the Dniepr were false.

While I listened to the news, Larion walked about in a state of agitation. It seemed that, since our decisions had been made, he was anxious to see me leave. I was anxious to leave as well. The issue had become too complicated for us to analyze; like in an old western, action was the only logical response. But, as no immediate action was possible, I chose to lounge about the flat in my underwear, drinking diluted vodka. Three thoughts kept entering and leaving my mind, like newspaper headings floating by in a stream. First one, then the next, then the next, then a blank space. The first was that this ennui was disrespectful to the power which I claimed to worship. The second was that I truly loved Larion and yet I *was* doing this. The third was that these two thoughts kept running through my mind.

The first thought worried me the most. Maybe this is

where any self-doubt is rooted; to recognize my state of mind as disrespectful suggested a closer affiliation with death than I previously warranted myself. I was able to have a correspondence of respect with death, and therefore I rose on a par with it, and this sort of thinking is vain. In order to acquire symbiosis, it is necessary to forget that it is attained through respect. To recognize sin is common, but to belabour the penalties of sin is disrespectful. Respect, then, in its cognitive structuring, is disrespectful. But even the third thought, that I had only two thoughts, returned me, like some mobius riddle, to the first thought.

I began to think of other things, how I would fill the remaining chapters of my life in Canada, how I could support a wife, whether I should feel at all obligated to. I thought of my health a lot as well, for I hadn't been back in Canada for almost a year now. Would they notice a change? Would I step through the security check and find I was a frail, hollow man? Or would I even make it through the check? Would the metal detector deplete me of my few remaining droplets of iron and send me crashing to the ground? The airport attendants with their tight, navy and light blue uniforms and their slick, phallic batons whoop-whooping over my dead body.

I knew nothing, really, about AIDS. The symptoms. Was my weakness a symptom? My windedness on coming up the stairwell? I know now they were. But also symptoms of a handful of other diseases. And what about Larion's swollen thyroid? Was this also a symptom? I know much more now, but at the time, had I been concerned for my petty life, I could have died of fear. Fear is disrespectful as well.

When I decided to think once again, and I know this sounds naïve but it was almost that deliberate a choice, when I decided to think, my mind ran rampant for a few days, latching onto everything and shaking it, shouting, "This here, I swear, this is a thought! And this! What a thought we have here!" Thought worked frenetically, sucking the sense from any wisp of an idea and then throwing it aside just as quickly. And the more I realized that I was losing control of my imagination, for it dawned on me that this was going on even while it was happening, the quicker my imagination worked to redeem itself, grabbing everything it crossed, searching desperately for a reason to exist, now that I had given it an opportunity. It finally settled down on a few particular notions. This may have constituted my most socially acceptable frame of mind during my entire stay in the Soviet Union. That should be a question on the form when one checks through customs. "What are you thinking?" "What three ideas are most prevalent in your mind today?" This would weed out the people with fear. And fear is not only disrespectful, but also dangerous.

So thoughts latched onto these ideas. The need to remain devoted to Larion until I died. The political dynamic between the BBC and the Soviet radio stations. And the sound of children. There were children, I had noticed, communicating on the sidewalk below our window all the time. We woke to the sound of bawling babies and nattering pre-schoolers as their mothers dragged them to daycare or, if the mother was a housewife, to do the morning grocery rounds: bakery, fruit store, meat store, dairy. Then it was the children from kindergarten, marching by on a field trip to one of these same stores, or to Lenin's Park (one of hundreds in the country), or to the community playground behind our building. At four o'clock, the school children passed by, singing and screaming, kicking and spitting, and then the day filled with a lull. The children were eating. The children were napping. The children were rushing through their homework so that they could go outside again and play road hockey, or marbles, or baseball. Actually, these are the games I played as a young boy; the boys in Kiev played badminton, soccer, and basketball.

The girls played games that they would never play as adults. Witches. Freeze Tag. Kick the Can. I played all these games myself, as a kid. I Declare War. We would draw a big circle on the ground and divide it into pie pieces—the world and its nations. If this computer did graphics I could draw it for you. There were no lakes or mountains or Lenin Parks in our world — just awkward, semi-triangular pieces of dirt. When it was your 'turn,' for you were polite and took turns at declaring war on each other, you counted to five while the other children left the planet. Then you threw the communal stick at one of the other players. If you hit them, you got to take a chunk of their nation as your own.

The object of the game, as you might know, was to take over the world. Except that, as children, we didn't see it as a representation of the world, though that is what we called it. And our pie pieces were not seen as nations. We gave them names like Blueberry or Hawaii, A&W or Ainsworth Hot Springs. Planets were popular — Venus, Neptune, Pluto. "I declare war on Uranus! I declare war on . . . Mars!" though we never stopped to question whether anybody actually lived there, whether they cared if we conquered them or not, whether they recognized us as a segment of their society. The game ended when it got too dark to keep playing. If, on the rare occasion, somebody actually succeeded in taking over the entire world, then a new world was drawn.

I hung out the window of our flat, sipping my vodka, watching the kids below me like a god. My drunken elevation seemed to please Larion. It made it easier for him to brood. He had gone to volunteer his help to the workers of Chernobyl and, when the Bureau of Civic Affairs told him no such system of aid existed, he sent them a letter stating that he had organized the Society to Aid the Workers of Chernobyl, OBPORACHERN, and was looking for volunteers. He included a stack of applications that he had mimeographed at the institute. Since he had no medical training (that would come with army service), he wasn't clear what to ask for. We thought up numerous questions, making a sort of game of it. In the end, all his questionnaire demanded was the volunteer's name, age, address, party rank, relevant skills, and allergies. When I left Kiev, Larion was still waiting for some response. Larion's notice of military duty still had not arrived but he sensed that it was imminent and was confident of his desire to serve. Something about Chernobyl had given him a sense of ambition. Maybe just the idea that there was something which needed to be done in the nation and which he was willing to do. He had been raised to serve but, up until now, there had been nothing to dish out, no way to challenge his potential. He was worried that the swelling near his thyroid gland might prohibit him from military duty and he walked about the apartment with a washcloth soaked in camomile tea tied to the side of his neck, a cure suggested by his aunt in Tbilisi. The swelling itself was not noticeable.

The morning of the day of my departure, I was quite drunk, but we managed to have sex one final time. In this, also, there was a sense of duty. But we were passionate and, when I finally came, we were both crying, which destroyed any sense of sincerity. Our emotions alienated us from the actions. We could see the inversion. It seemed to be our final mutual action and neither of us, it became clear, was sure we wanted it to be so. And it seemed unfortunate that it was *still* not too late. It would have been easier if the consul had clubbed me in the night and driven me to Moscow in the trunk of a car. But the waiting, waiting, made it seem like our mutual devotion was insincere since neither of us was about to consider re-entering that sociopolitical quagmire once again.

The day was ugly, overcast, but with the streets white with dust and the air uncommonly humid. It made one want to leave the city. I left all my possessions at the flat except for my clothes, I.D., and some papers. The streets were full of families shopping and strolling along the boulevard. Trios of police officers sauntered up and down the sidewalks confidently. The chestnut trees rattled their branches, and the occasional young leaf broke free and eased into the crowd, where it was trampled. It was impossible for us to find a vacant taxi, with so many people out on the town. We shared a cigarette to kill the time, neither speaking nor looking at each other.

Departures are one of the few times when western culture demands that individuals be literate. "I hate goodbyes." "I never know what to say." "Let it not be goodbye, but 'paka.'" There is something wrong with this, but I'm not sure what. Here I am, typing all this into my computer, and when it comes to recording what it is we said to each other, the characters go mute. It's true though. Larion and I did not say a word. I remember us standing on the street corner, those gay crowds waltzing past us, the pastel facades which lined the street. I remember the tepid breeze winding itself around my throat, plunging down my shirt, shaking the dust off my pantlegs. The smell of bread from a nearby store. I remember the smell distinctly. The crowds were probably not as blissful as I remember them now. Maybe the smell of bread is actually part of another memory as well.

I felt lifted, at that particular moment, spirited upward, like a balloon tied to Larion's cuff. It seemed feasible that I could remain in Kiev then, living with Larion, doing whatever I would do in Canada, but living with Larion. That was the closest I came. But he would be joining the army. Land Manoeuvres. He preferred this, he said, over Aviation. And who am I trying to kid? Or have I answered that one already? The soles of my feet touched the sidewalk just as a taxi pulled up beside us.

We were silent during the ride to the train station as well, Larion and I sitting on either side of the back seat, my khaki Army & Navy knapsack between us. He tapped his knee, sharply defined through his pale jeans. His fingers reminded me of the limp candles at the Organ Concert Hall, milky orange, thin and bent. Larion did not turn to look at me, and my gaze never left him. I was worried that if I turned away, even for a moment, he would disappear. A balloon is sucked out the window. A cat shoots out the door. And again, at the station platform, it took so fucking long. That's funny, a day too long for a person with AIDS; though it makes perfect sense when I think about it. We watched two children playing with thin, naked caterpillars that had infested a nearby bush. The leaves had almost all been eaten, but there was no other vegetation nearby, so the insects clung to the bare branches which had been their sustenance until then. I remember my father killing this same type of insect (they never become butterflies), spraying tractor gas through the perforated nozzle of a pressure pump. The green worms dropped onto the grass in clumps, writhing like itchy dogs. Or maybe these types do become butterflies; I'm not sure. The boy and girl had been picking the bugs off the leaves and stuffing them into their pockets, but then their mother noticed what they were doing and dragged them away by their sleeves.

Larion's greasy bangs hung over his eyes and a bread crumb clung to his night's growth of beard. His lips pushed against mine and the oily, blue lights cast a plastic pallor over his forehead and cheekbones. I boarded before necessary. He walked parallel to me as I made my way to my seat. I could see him on the platform whenever I passed a compartment with an open door. That sensation creeping up on me.

The glass of my open window was the green of old Kerr canning jars. I told him I would write from Moscow and he said he would be at his aunt's but that he would find the letter when he got back. The last of the travellers boarded the train now. Wealthy families. Many kids dressed in dark blue. A grandmother chewing. All quiet. And that sensation returning, "too soon, too soon." The train began sliding out of the station, almost subversively, like a fried egg out of a pan, or a harp seal off of ice. Too soon. What am I doing? Why? "Get in!" I shouted. "Get in the train!" He waved his arm at me, casting the idea off as if it were a spider web that had crossed his face.

"If you stick your neck out, you'll get killed." It was an attendant who offered this wise advice. When I turned back to the open window, the train had already left the station. I was overcome by a weary regret. Why was life taking so long? It is as clear now, sitting here typing through the night, as it had been then that I will never feel remorse for having killed Larion or Bogdon. Nor will I ever feel that my actions wholly originated in my discovering that I was terminally ill. And now I know that HIV positive does not mean exactly that. AIDS did nothing but add precision to intentions which had already been formulated, nothing but precision and access to means. It presented me with an alternative to a social structure that wanted me dead. It was as if I had been suddenly thrust upon the acme of that hierarchy, had become the disseminator of death, given the power to choose with whom I would rule and abide.

I have wanted my own ever since they began denying it to me. But as a standard individual, there was no way for me to achieve any real change. I was so aware of my own mortality that I had no patience for gradual developments, and this impatience had rendered me impotent. It was not an issue of reforming *them*; I had no care for them whatsoever. What I wanted most at that moment, sitting in my compartment, letting my eyes follow the white line of the horizon, was to be left alone with my comrades, my family — alone alone with Larion. This was probably the first time I had questioned my convictions.

During the train trip I half-expected Larion to enter the compartment, half-expected the porter I had met on the train the year before. I knew that the appearance of either of them would alleviate my scratch of doubt. Or if death would only remove this impatient wait. I followed the flow of the gently folding fields, slashed by flashes of telephone poles that, because of their awkward angles, seemed to have been thrust into the ground by some unconcerned god. My eyes were led by the steady swoop, swoop of loose telephone wires. The darkening sky. The sparks of porch lights, precious amber in the matte black screen of night. I was the only one in my compartment, so I had a smoke. All this time I continued waiting for some external activity, something to counter the hair-line of doubt which had fallen across my mind. My small room was constrictive, demanding patience. It seemed that, during this moment of transference, I could hear the silent inactivity of the world, the lack of response to my actions. The homes had disappeared and it was pitch black outside except for the light from my compartment hitting the tracks. The train was silent as well, coasting to Moscow, the quick rhythm coming not from the wheels over the tracks but from the impatient pacing of my own mind. I had another smoke. I stared out the window for maybe another hour. It was not until I arranged my jacket into a pillow, turned out the light, and lay myself down, that I began to cry.

11

We took a taxi to my mother-in-law's. I met her. I have nothing against her but I hope she does not enter this text again. In Moscow, I tried to return to my earlier vision. "The map of my death had been spread out before me." Oh well, it will do as an introduction. It's what I've been asked to talk about. But it must be clear that by this time, not so long ago now, it was hard to think anything so precise. The only urgency was one of waiting. After calling Paul and arranging with him to find me an apartment and meet me at the airport, I feigned fatigue and went to bed, much to the disappointment of my wife, who wanted to show me the three crates of Georgian wool, the choir of matrooshkas, and the other gifts her mother had bought us as wedding presents. Life, it was clear to me, was not as obvious as I had thought. I felt like I was loitering.

I always knew death was not the antithesis of life, but I had always felt life had an antithesis, some undefined opposite that made it less entire than death, and now I was not sure. Life was the unclear concept that had no options. Yet, to live was only possible if one believed in life's impermanence. We could never admit that we have no fucking clue what we are doing here. Is it true that death is really the only hope we have of ever figuring this out? Why, if life is so useless, will it not let me go? Weekend wordgames. Weakened.

So here it was, time for the Big Out, me and a woman I didn't love packing bags for Ca-Na-Da, one little two little three Canadians. Everything doesn't work in threes. Or even twos for that matter. One of us was bumped our seat to a dignitary. My wife would have to arrive a day after me.

The Vancouver airport was chaos when I arrived. The entire city was teeming with Expo tourists and subdued young men wheeling around obscure pieces of electrical equipment. I went into the washroom to see if my hair looked the same as it had a year ago, and then went to find Paul, who was sitting comfortably in the reception area, slowly ruffling the dog-eared pages of *Time*, scratching his neck absent-mindedly.

He did not notice me immediately so I sat down beside him and picked up a magazine, though my eyes did not leave his face. It was an awkward moment, the levels of affection demanding redefinition due to the long absence, the absence itself having altered these levels of affection, and I was unsure if I still loved him. When he smiled, and it was clear his eyes had not changed, I loved him as much as always. The word 'love' is being used often here because my feelings for Paul were less pure and entire than the feelings I still had, and will always have, for Larion. It was momentarily disconcerting to realize that Paul would necessarily join Larion and me, that all those who died would. But then I caught my assumptive-ness, and relaxed. My separation from Larion was such a physical process that it was not a relevant separation at all. I continue to exist only because he does and I have no doubt that our earthly deaths will be a single transition. My reunion with Paul, on the other hand, was physically uncomfortable because I only *loved* him and therefore had to use the social languages to communicate.

We hugged, which, to observers, meant that Paul and I were two dear friends reunited. We kissed each other on the lips, which meant we were either brothers, lovers, or mutual friends of someone recently deceased. I squeezed his thigh through the rough silk of his trousers and he squeezed my crotch, which meant we were lovers indeed and nobody had died. I was struck by that final image of Larion, pale on the pale grey platform, smiling, the entire silver sky glowing, his lanky arm swiping as if to stroke a horse's flank. The air was warm that day. We wore our coats unbuttoned and our sleeves rolled. This is how I remembered it then.

It was during the short walk to the luggage check that I realized that more than Paul's external appearance had deteriorated. He walked slowly, breathed heavily, and carried himself as if he were holding back a shit. The thirty-minute wait for my possessions left him worn out and we parted for the day. I was hesitantly jealous. I wanted to ask him how long he had, but I was sure he would not understand my excitement. At my flat, a spacious two bedroom with high ceilings, hardwood floors, located in a dark skyscraper with the chosen view of False Creek, I unpacked my wife's luggage in search of a coffee cup. Besides the flood of gaudy Ukrainian souvenirs and piles of clothing and memorabilia which I could not chide her for, she had also packed a milk steamer, about a dozen balls of yarn, and a book on the making of Chinese paper. The only dishes were a set of silver egg spoons and a rubber beer cooler in the shape of a pineapple. The water in the West End tastes like a dentist's office.

The first thing I did was go to the Soviet Consulate to see if they were aware that my wife was moving to Canada. As it turned out, the consulate had not been aware and saw no reason why they should be. But they asked me to bring her by the following day so that they could familiarize her with their facilities and the various Russian and Ukrainian organizations in the Lower Mainland. The consuls were more interested in finding out what exactly had gone on in Chernobyl, since their radio did not reach Soviet stations and Moscow only told them what they were willing to have foreigners hear. I was unable to give them any new information although they informed me of the deterioration of the ozone layer caused by the nuclear event. They also gave detailed information on the greenhouse effect, what signs to watch for, and what exactly the life after would be like. This was all couched in vivid descriptions appropriated from a recently released American movie set in the Australian outback and starring a '60s Motown singer as the leader of a cannibalistic commune. The person who saw me out reminded me to visit "Soviet Pavilion of Expo '86" and pierced my lapel with a pin bearing the image of the Soviet and Canadian flags entwined.

I ate dinner at a Vietnamese restaurant on Davie Street which had an Expo display called "The Earth Is So Close to Everybody." I decided to take a walk to Stanley Park and it wasn't until then that I realized Paul had chosen to plant me and my wife in the centre of Vancouver's homosexual community, and this amused me. Everything would continue celebrating life regardless of my apathy to it. Paul, even though AIDS had withered him dry, continued to see death as the source of his suffering rather than his deliverance. Paul's desperation affirmed my own control. AIDS made revenge obsolete.

Though the sun was low in the sky, its rays were sharp, like the glare of my computer screen in the darkness. The sky was stark blue, the colour of Auntie Margo's swimming pool, kidney-shaped and rimmed with huge granite stones (which she always called garnet). Auntie Margo had died young, when her parka got tangled in the back gears of her husband's, my uncle's, skidoo. A sort of Canadian Isadora Duncan. Isadora had managed to live okay in the Soviet Union, married to Esenin. But then, he had committed suicide. I must keep my mind from working its way back to the Soviet Union. It does that all the time; sometimes I forget I'm in Canada.

And I was wrong. The coast is not like the Ukraine. At least not in Vancouver, not in Stanley Park. I took off my bomber and let the cool wind tighten my skin. As soon as I got there I took the footpath from English Bay that leads through the pine trees and to the lake. It was relaxing to hear the quiet scratching and gnawing of Canadian birds and rodents. The lake shone like a plate of mercury in the descending night. In the blurred silence, I could make out the image of two men fornicating nearby. I had forgotten that this was where we came. I had also forgotten that it was unsafe for a man to wander in the dim purity of the park alone, since gangs of fag bashers often hid in the bushes waiting to hammer home their views. Western society's retribution for our pathetic, sublunar freedom. I stepped into the darkness, my black silhouette on the dark pines in the new night.

It was then that I made my final stroll along those twisted paths through the pine trees, which were really the last paths of our inner fusion and, I admit it now, the paths of my need. Larion had been ignominious during my last days in Kiev and that is the main reason I worship him now. It does not matter whether he saw his actions as sacrificial (for that is exactly what they were), as long as the actions had been carried out. His impatience, his insolence, his igneous temper, were each like balms to me. And like bombs, he knew. Having decided to stay in the Soviet Union, he had passed through that same physical ache alone, while I spun within my own selfishness.

I was just about to type that he forgave me but it was not forgiveness, because my crime, the crime of selfishness, was contained within the realm of our fusion. Forgiveness is within the fusion, is simultaneous with the crime, just as love is within our union and therefore not the definition of it. Words! I try to write everything knowing that my words lie in the juxtaposition of dead colours, everything as it wriggles just before being pinned to the page.

The next morning my bedroom was painfully dry. The heat rising from the street made the buildings outside my window shimmer and the harsh light defined everything with an unnecessary clarity. It was as if I were being born into a world of sharp objects and harsh noises. With my eyes closed,

I could see deep violet and a thin red line, like a scratch or some wounded animal's trail of blood. I dressed and caught a taxi to the airport.

I was early, so I went to the can and looked at myself in the mirror to see if I was vibrant — for Paul, not for my wife. And I did look sort of youngish actually — hair tousled, jeans torn, sneakers worn (the ones from Kiev, because I thought they would make a stunning touch when I told Paul the story). Pale, and thinner. No, maybe not. I must be thinner. I found a twenty-five-cent weigh scale and weighed myself; I had gained ten pounds over the year. I bought a pair of sunglasses at a boutique. It was a new west coast summer and I was ready to die.

I just asked my wife and she said I had looked vibrant when she got off the plane. And not pale (but then, compared to her). So no, I guess I can't think of any definite signs of degeneration. The most ambiguous aspect of this illness, it seems to me, for those who care to know, is how difficult it is to tell whether you have the symptoms. And how easy it is to cast your symptoms aside as just, oh, nothing, it'll pass. Like a loss of breath. Like pimples or bumps that don't go away, or take a long time to do so. And then for women, any menstrual peculiarity may be a sign, or this is what they've found. And of course geography doesn't make a difference anymore either. My mother might be HIV positive, for kissing the scrape of my sister's ex-boyfriend's kid.

The first *Vancouver Province* I had read in a year, over coffee in the airport café, did not mention AIDS. A cure, of course, would have cast me back into the mire. Instead, the paper was full of articles on Expo, summer sports, and various environmental crossfires. The paper lacked the political content I had grown accustomed to in Kiev; even the cartoons were not entertaining since they didn't relate to any real issues. Only the obituaries and birth columns gave me any pleasure, and this was only voyeuristic. "Smile of the Day," with its intimate details of a citizen's likes and dislikes, was also interesting, for the same reason, as were most of the articles in the paper's "Life" section. The centre spread was on Native Indian jade miniatures of B.C. Place stadium, which were "selling like hotcakes." I tore out an article on a gallery opening of works by three young artists who claimed Futurism and Suprematism as their sources of inspiration. The quote under the grainy reproduction of Malevich's "White On White" read "all reference to ordinary objective life has been left behind and nothing is real except feeling . . . the feeling of nonobjectivity." The last paragraph of the article stated that a bookstore next to the gallery had caught fire and therefore the show was postponed. This seemed ironic, the objective elements intruding on these nonobjectivists.

I loaded my wife and her baggage into a taxi and, after dropping off her stuff at the flat, took her to the consulate. At first she protested, saying she wanted to sleep, but I said it was urgent bureaucracy. After finally ridding myself of her (You're saying, "Is she there while he's typing this? Can he really be such a prick?" but yes, I am, and why not? Do you recall why I married her? Can you imagine what she reminds me of now? "Upsy daisy," and I want to punch her in the face. But I can't now, after what we've done. The new life is important to me for some reason. I'll be the last one to ask why. I can see her, just out of the corner of my eye, sitting in the recliner reading *Western Living* and picking at that little mole on her earlobe, looking as content as a pregnant cat.) So yes, after finally ridding myself of her, I rushed over to Kitsilano to meet Paul.

He finally showed up, as I've described already, and our meeting would have been a failure, if not for the brashness of Johnny Cash's illegitimate daughter. When she finally brought us our meals, she winked at Paul again and, when he did not respond, she snapped, "What's with you?" Her coarseness confused him for a moment, so she giggled, saying, "Oh skip it, I forgive you," as she walked away, whipping her thick, orange hair over her shoulder with exaggerated flare. It all aggravated me — the waitress, Nana Mouskouri singing "It's a Small World" through the speakers which hung from opposite corners of the room, my sour Greek omelette.

"Aren't you hungry? You've got to keep up your appetite." Paul cut off a piece of his omelette with his butter knife, peppered it, brushed it over the dollop of ketchup on the side of his plate and slipped it into his thin-lipped mouth. He ate as if each mouthful of scrambled egg were an aesthetic delight. The bump on his neck, which I had always taken to be a birthmark, was actually a wart. I could see the black dots where his bronzer had rubbed off.

"My appetite's fine. The food just has a bit more bite than I like."

"Regardless, my specialist said that even if eating becomes a chore, one has to maintain a regular diet. People with AIDS often say they have no appetite even though their real reason for not eating is that they can't bother with the hassle."

"How did you know I'm positive? Does it show?"

"Actually, no, it doesn't show. I was surprised to find you so . . . robust." He referred to my body as if he'd come across it earlier that morning, while taking out the garbage or something. Still spicing each mouthful of omelette individually, chewing slowly, steadily, like a cow. The rise and fall of those urbane jaws — ur bane ur bane ur bane. His composure irritated me. A fat, blue bottle fly landed on my glass of milk and walked along the inner edge, pushing its face against the glass like a dog on a scent.

"So then how did you know? Who told you?"

"Nobody had to tell me. I gave it to you." The fly slid down the milky sides of the glass into the opaque, white liquid. It lay on its back, drifting on a current without any apparent source.

"You let me go to the Soviet Union, knowing I might die there?"

"It seemed like the perfect opportunity for me to let you figure it out on your own. I didn't want to interfere in your coming to terms with it. I imagined you as dead when you got on the plane. I never knew I'd given it to you until it was too late, or at least I was pretty sure it was. Understand I hadn't expected either of us to make it this long. But with AZT and all, I've stopped expecting anything. We may be here forever. There's a fly in your milk."

Another dollop, another mouthful. Ur bane ur bane ur bane.

"You're aware that your speech would sound entirely maniac to anyone else?"

"Not to me," said the waitress who was pouring coffee for a couple in the booth behind me. She scratched her left breast with long, unpolished nails. "He's been talking like this for months. It's a self-sufficiency group he's in. It makes perfect sense to me now, if I let myself think that way. But I won't. I thought that way all day Friday and, on Saturday, I couldn't get out of bed. There was no reason.

"I figure it's sort of like play-acting." She had come over to our table and was standing, arms crossed, gazing out at the beach thoughtfully. "Or it's like being a right-wing fundamentalist. I do that sometimes too. Especially when they start clammering about another hackneyed movie which says something about Christians. I start wearing sweaters and speaking seriously to everybody, my mailman. But that only lasts a couple of days. I can act like Paul for weeks on end. Laying in bed with a scarf on. Sometimes I call my friends and tell them to visit me." Paul chuckled like a conspiratorial urchin, a pursed smile clinging to his bowed head. The waitress began writing out our bill.

"I guess you know Expo celebrations have started," Paul said, to fill the silence which ensued as we waited for the waitress to leave.

"Downtown is swarming with tourists," I acknowledged. "Even the Vietnamese restaurant I went to yesterday had a carousel of brochures."

"There's fireworks in False Creek tonight," said the waitress, acting excited and pushing back her glasses. "You should go watch them. I'm being myself right now. Really. I love fireworks. The Catherine Wheels are awesome. The Lava Spit and the Chinese Crackers!"

"Ohh," said Paul, sounding like Alice at the tea party ("Come, we shall have some fun now!"). And his child-like joy making me feel like a prodigal son. I agreed with Paul to have him over to watch the fireworks from our balcony that evening. The waitress refilled our cups and then Paul and I watched the beach crowd and waited for evening. "This is the best time of day. All the young boys start coming off the beach to get ready for a night out." I stirred my coffee and looked out at the sky, waiting for it to darken. The white shoreline was packed with copper men, sun-stoned children, and young couples consummating their love with sandy fingers and moist lips. A young boy and girl were trying to flip a small, grey crab into their sand pail with the aid of some popsicle sticks. The crab finally clutched onto one of the sticks and stopped moving. The little boy cautiously took hold of the other end of the stick, lifted the animal over the pail of water and, with a squeal of success, let go.

Sailboats and windsurfers slid in spastic lines like water spiders across the white ripples of the bay. I could make out the white houses of North Vancouver in the distance, clinging to the Lions like prehistoric mollusks under the heat of an indifferent sun. The Lions themselves, superior as sphinxes, ignored both the flimsy abodes clustered at their feet and the lacteal clouds swirling around their heads in the setting sky.

Rather than hating Paul for directing me, I have to thank him for his creation of what is clearly my ultimate earthly event, my only glimpse above the waves of this dark, mediocre reality. And since it's only the structure of perception that I can be concerned with here, and not social justification, my pleasure, which I can feel rising even now, just thinking about Paul's involvement, celebrates the worthlessness my life has had in the viewpoint of others. It makes me thankful that reality is so mundane. How easy it has been to step above it. Paul had been correct in perceiving me as dead when I left to the Soviet Union. As far as he was concerned, I was dead, at least for that year. This is even how I perceive, and represent, myself. This is analogous with my acceptance of Larion's death, which I couldn't have handled if not for the fact that I contributed to it, in my own little way. Somehow I know that he, at least, has died by now, and hasn't had to wait.

It is useless to conjecture what I might have felt if I were in some way alive. I am dead to Paul, and dead to myself, and, most importantly, dead to Larion, who is myself. Nothing is repeated in that sentence. There is no doubt that, since my being depends on a fusion which allows me to be a voyeur of my own self, I am utterly dead. The condemned is dead, just as we say that a volcano which has lain silent, has not shot forth its froth and lava for centuries, is dead. And it *is* dead, and remains dead, until one dark evening it begins to fill with heat, to steam and whistle above the muted hills which coil about its feet. It stirs, rises, explodes in a defiant display of hot froth and spits of sparks amidst a shroud of black clouds and the darkness of night. And then lies dead once more.

How we write geography, how we talk about its lives and deaths. Or shelf life. Or active life. This is all such a reassurance to me. It is how I have always seen. I had intended on giving the pertinent history of my life here, but it seems to me that my history began, maybe ended, before I did. I haven't said much about what I've been doing since my return to Canada. Or who I've been doing it with. But that can't interest you; it would all amount to nothing but that final, thin banner of smoke. I still don't know what else to do but wait. I've presented my concerns, what I define as my life and, though much of it might be unexplained, this is the place to end. Knowing these are the last words I intend to type onto the screen, I am drawn once again toward requesting vindication. But I don't expect it. And in reality I feel nothing but tired. The dawn is here; I can see the ocean and the white sky getting gradually lighter, like two sheets of paper separating. My family has gone to sleep and the sand has begun to finally fill my eyes as well.

 DENNIS DENISOFF's fiction and poetry has appeared in such publications as *Writing, Fiddlehead, Canadian Fiction Magazine, West Coast line,* and in the anthology *East of Main* (Arsenal Pulp, 1989). In 1985-86, he studied at the Kiev Pedagogical Institute of Foreign Languages; currently, he is a doctoral student in English at McGill University in Montreal.